BLOODY GORY TALES

I was born at the height of The Troubles in Northern Ireland, the eldest child of four. In 1978 I attended the Abby Primary School in Newry. The teachers there tried to drum the curriculum into us but I was just a poor student all through school life. Then I left school and was just interested in having a good time, until I met my soon-to-be wife. A couple of years after that my children started to arrive. I used to make up bedtime stories for them. That's when my wife told me I had a knack for telling short stories.

BLOODY GORY TALES

D. B. McSloy

BLOODY GORY TALES

Olympia Publishers
London

www.olympiapublishers.com
OLYMPIA PAPERBACK EDITION

A CIP catalogue record for this title is
available from the British Library.

ISBN: 978-1-84897-203-2

This is a work of fiction.
Names, characters, places and incidents originate from the writer's
imagination. Any resemblance to actual persons, living or dead, is purely
coincidental.

First Published in 2012

Olympia Publishers
60 Cannon Street
London
EC4N 6NP

Printed in Great Britain

Dedication

To William Bunkham
1949-2012

Another ray of sunshine taken from our world

THE BUTTER KNIFE MURDERS

1971. A six-year-old boy sits in front of the television watching his favourite programme. In the background his mother and father fight as usual. The little boy turns the volume up to drown out the voices of his angry parents.

A knock comes to the front door. No one hears but the little boy. The boy gets up from the floor and goes to the kitchen where his parents are still fighting.

He tries to tell them there's somebody at the door. The young boy's father grabs him and lifts him by the arms then throws him onto the chair in the living room.

"What did I tell you about interrupting me and your mother?" his father asked angrily. The boy looked at his father with his eyes filling with tears his father looked back with a sorrowful expression. "Sorry son I didn't mean to yell, be a good boy and sit and watch your programme."

His father then went back to the kitchen and his parents began to argue. A moment later there was another knock at the door. The boy ran to the kitchen door to tell his parents then he remembered his father was very angry the last time he interrupted.

He walked towards the front door. As he reached it there was a third knock, the little boy put his small hand on the handle and opened the door.

He looked out and saw a man. The man stooped down and asked with a large smile on his face, "Is your mommy or daddy home little fellow?"

The little boy pointed towards the kitchen. The man, still with a smile on his face, rustled the boy's hair and stood up. He walked into the hall and stooped down again. The man put his finger over the child's lips and went, "SHHHH. There's a good boy," in a soft and friendly voice.

The man cocked his head to one side and smiled, "I'm going to speak to your mommy and daddy now." The man stood up and reached into his jacket and took out a large homemade knife. He walked towards the kitchen where the couple were fighting. He opened the door and walked in. The man closed the door behind him. The small boy immediately ran over to the door and opened it. As he looked in he watched the man stab his father in the chest. His father dropped to the floor and the boy's stunned mother started to scream.

The man walked slowly over to the screaming woman with the homemade knife dripping with her husband's blood down by his side. The little boy stood in the doorway, his eyes wide-open, tears streaming down his face, unable to help his mother and paralysed with fear.

The only thing the boy could do was watch as the man with his free hand grabbed his mother by the throat and slammed her down onto the kitchen table.

The man stroked the woman's face with his blood-soaked blade, "SHHHHH. Be a good girl now," he said with a quiet and calm voice. The young boy's mother lay still and ridged, she begged the man not to hurt her.

He put his left arm across her chest and looked at her face then smiled, then with the knife in his right hand he plunged it into her lower abdomen.

She took a deep breath and tried to scream but she couldn't. The man slid the sharp blade of the knife slowly up her stomach. She turned to her son as she choked on her own blood and she stretched out her arm and mouthed, "Help me."

The boy could see the life drain from his mother's eyes. The man stood up straight and walked over to the sink, where he washed his hands and then dried them. Then he turned and walked over to the small boy and stooped down. The man smiled and said, "Your mommy was like butter."

He pinched the boy's cheek, "You're a good boy," the man said happily. Then he stood up and walked towards the front door.

As he got to the hallway the door was kicked in by two policemen. They saw the blood over his clothes and rushed him. A third officer walked towards the living room and saw the young boy staring into the kitchen as the officer walked over to the boy he called out, "You alright kid?"

The child turned around to the officer and pointed into the kitchen with his eyes wide open. He says only one word, "Mommy."

The officer looked into the kitchen and saw what the man had done. He turned away, lifted the child then carried him out to the squad car.

39 years later, 2010

7:30 in the morning the alarm woke Robert from another unrestful sleep. Hearing the loud irritating noise, he awkwardly searched the nightstand to turn the alarm off.

He arose slowly and put his bare feet on the cold laminated floor, then he then stretched and yawned.

When he stood up he shuffled across the room to the bathroom. He stood at the washbasin and looked into the mirror at his reflection and thought to himself, "Man, I look like crap." He took a shave and a wash then went to his closet and opened the door, there were clothes everywhere.

"What a mess," he thought and then shook his head. He searched through the mountain of garments and found a half descent pair of jeans and a wrinkled shirt. He took a deep sniff of the shirt and grunted "It'll have to do."

He got dressed and made himself a pot of coffee and sat at the table to drink it. He reached for his wallet and opened it. He stared intensely at his detective's badge. Robert was a cop who came from a long line of cops. He thought that the people in power tied his hands and he couldn't do his job properly. He was often frustrated.

He thought to himself as he looked at his badge I should quit. The fucking criminals get more protection from the law than the victims, then he sighed.

He closed his wallet and started to drink his coffee when someone knocked on his door. Robert roared, "Who is it?"

A deep voice sounded from the other side of the door, "Open up cop I'm going to fucking kill you."

Robert slowly got up from the chair and edged himself to the coat rack beside the door. He grasped his gun from the tan shoulder holster that was hanging on the rack. He gripped the weapon firmly with his right hand and with his left hand he swung the door open. "Jesus Mathews, don't shoot," came a nervous sounding voice from the dimly-lit hallway. Robert stood in the doorway with his hand trembling and his eyes wide open. He could feel his heart pounding through his chest.

"It's me you stupid fucker, man I almost crapped my shorts." It was Phil McCann, Robert's partner and best friend. Phil is an outstanding officer and he boasts he keeps Robert out of trouble. He's a little cocky but he's a good man to have around in a fight.

Robert: "You're an asshole McCann, one of these days someone is going to put a bullet in you for doing shit like that. What are you doing here at this time of the morning anyway?"

Phil: "Come on Robert don't be a pussy, it was only a joke. Anyway Murphy wants us down at the station asap."

Robert: "There must be something wrong if Murphy asked for us, you know he hates us, did he tell you what was up."

Phil: "He didn't tell me a thing, all I know is that he sounded very agitated. And by the way, it's you he hates, not me."

Robert and Phil left the apartment, headed to the car and drove to the station. When they got there things were unusually busy. Murphy came out of the office, "Mathews, McCann get over here."

Murphy is the precinct captain, a man in his early 50s, he likes to think he's old school but in truth he's a man that likes to get his face on TV and likes to take the credit for every crime solved in this city. He's not well liked or respected. Many people think he got where he is today by kissing ass.

Phil: "Top of the morning captain, what are you doing here so early this fine morning?" he joked sarcastically.

Murphy: "No one likes a smart ass McCann now shut the fuck up and listen. One of our own has gone missing. He's been gone for three days. His partner went to his apartment, the place has been turned over and he found dried blood stains on the floor. I want you two to find him."

"Who was it?" asked Robert.

"Grant," answered Murphy.

Robert: "Were there any witnesses to any disturbance on the day he went missing?"

Murphy: "The man that lives next door to Grant. Him and Grant didn't get on."

"What's this guy's name?" asked Phil.

Murphy looked at a paper on his desk, "Arthurs, Peter Arthurs."

Phil: "Ok captain we'll go interview Arthurs and then we'll check out Grant's place."

Robert and Phil drove to Peter Arthurs' home. They stepped out of the car and looked around.

Phil: "Look at this place, how Grant was able to afford a place like this is beyond me."

They walked into the apartment building and went up to the fourth floor Robert knocked on Arthurs' apartment door. A few moments later a small thin man opened the door.

"Yes, can I help?" he asked with a wispy little voice.

Robert and Phil produced their identification. "Mr. Arthurs?" asked Robert.

"Yes," answered Arthurs.

"I'm detective Mathews and this is detective McCann would you mind if we come in and ask you a few questions?"

Arthurs: "Yes of course come in. It's about time you got here, I called you three days ago."

"You did Mr. Arthurs, about what?" asked Phil.

"Mr. Grant next door. I'm not one for complaining but Grant had another party I've asked him time and time again to turn the noise down but he just laughed in my face. Three nights ago I just came to the end of my tether and rung you guys."

Phil: "You've misunderstood Mr. Arthurs, we're here to investigate the disappearance of Officer Grant."

"I swear detectives I had nothing to do with any disappearance, all I did was call the police and complain about the noise," Arthurs said a worried tone.

Robert: "Don't worry Mr. Arthurs we don't suspect you of anything we need to know about the night you made the complaint, like what did you hear and see."

Arthurs: "I didn't see anything but I heard music then a knock at his door. There were raised voices some crashes, but that was nothing new, I heard things like that all the time. That's it, that's all I know."

They thanked Mr. Arthurs for all his help and left.

Robert and Phil went next door and they let themselves in to Grant's apartment.

Phil: "Jesus, look at this place."

"I know, it's a mess," replied Robert.

Phil: "No I mean look at it, a cop couldn't afford to live here with the salary we get. Look at the bloodstain, there wasn't a lot spilt for Grant to have been carried out dead. He either walked out on his own or was dragged out but I think he was still alive."

Robert and Phil left Grant's apartment and walked to the car. A message came in on the radio for them to go to the docks right away. When they got there the place had been closed off.

The captain saw them getting out of the car and shouted to them.

Murphy: "McCann, Mathews, over here."

They walked over to where Murphy was standing. "Why the urgency, captain?" asked Robert.

Murphy: "You can stop looking for Grant, we found him, he's over there, someone had a grand old time with him," he said nervously. "Jack's over there, now go and speak to him."

Jack Kent was the head pathologist. He was a good friend of Robert and Phil's. Jack was a big man with an unusually bright outlook on life.

Robert and Phil walked over to Jack. "You well, Jack?" asked Robert. "You don't look you're usual cheery self today."

Jack: "I was having a fine day until I saw the mess someone made of Grant here, look." Jack pulled back the sheet, Robert and Phil looked down at Grant's body.

Robert let out a loud gulp when he saw Grant's beaten and mutilated corpse. He asked, with a horrified look on his face, "What the fuck happened here."

Jack: "As you can see he took a bad beating which seemed to have been given around a two day period. It was the beating that killed him then he was moved here. This is where the mutilation was done."

"So he was killed elsewhere then moved here and then the assailant stuck around and did the rest. How do you know it didn't all happen here?" asked Phil.

Jack: "If it had been done here there would have been a lot more blood. The killer then took this, what looks like a homemade knife, and inserted the weapon into Grant's lower abdomen. He started to cut and didn't stop till he hit the stomach."

"That's sick, this fuck's not all there in the head," added Phil.

"And the person who owns this boat is going to be sick when he sees the state it's in," Robert commented.

Jack: "I doubt it, you're looking at the owner, its Grant's boat. There's pictures of him all over the place and there's something else." They followed Jack into the boat and on the wall there was written .GRANT WAS LIKE BUTTER.

"He did that with a piece off Grant's liver."

Phil: "What the fuck does 'he was like butter' mean?"

Robert: "I've heard that somewhere before."

"Where?" asked Phil.

Robert: "I can't remember it sounds familiar I've heard it somewhere before. It doesn't matter."

They stepped off the boat and walked towards the captain. "Well what do you think?" asked Murphy.

Robert: "Something doesn't smell right about this whole thing, I think we should look into Grant's bank accounts and check into his associates we can speak to his partner, maybe he may know something."

Murphy: "Are you saying Grant was dirty?"

Phil thought to himself, "Why did Murphy jump to that conclusion? We never said that Grant was dirty."

"Well, you're wrong he was a good friend, and so is Cole," Murphy said angrily.

"Who is Cole?" asked Robert.

Murphy: "Dan Cole, Grant's partner."

Phil: "Robert's right, how did Grant get the money for that apartment and the boat it would have cost a wad of cash."

"Never mind how he got the cash just find out who killed him. You're not going to drag a highly decorated officer's name into the gutter because of a suspicion," Murphy roared with a loud irritated voice.

Phil: "Are you telling us you're hindering our investigation so your friend's name can stay clean? What are you trying to protect, Grant's name or your reputation? You couldn't have a bent cop under your command, let alone a friend, isn't that right Murphy?"

Murphy: "You'll do what I tell you to, and I'm Captain Murphy to you, or if you can't manage that, 'Sir' will do. You understand McCann?" he said with a sarcastic tone.

Phil: "Yes, sir," he said sarcastically. "But we will be checking into Grant's finances and if you have a problem with that we can take it over your head."

"Fine," said Murphy, "do all the checking you want, but I want to be kept informed." Then he angrily stamped off.

Robert and Phil drove back to the station and Phil contacted Officer Cole.

Phil: "Cole will be here soon. I'll talk to him while you get what we need on Grant."

A short while later Cole walked into the squad room and approached Phil's desk. "You want to talk to me, detective?" asked Cole.

"Yes, officer Cole. Lets go somewhere a bit more private," said Phil and led Cole to one of the interview suites.

Phil: "Officer Cole, let me start off by extending my condolences, by all accounts your partner was a fine officer. I'm sorry but I have to ask you some questions."

"That's ok, I understand," said Cole.

Phil: "When was the last time you saw your partner?"

Cole: "About four days ago after our shift was over we left the station. I asked him if he wanted to go for a drink. He said 'no' and that he was tired and he was heading straight home."

Phil: "What way did he seem when you parted company?"

Cole: "He was alright, the same as usual."

Phil: "Can you tell me how Jimmy could afford to live in that apartment and that boat must have cost at least a couple of hundred grand."

Cole: "What are you saying? You think Jimmy was on the take, detective? With all due respect, go fuck yourself." Cole stood up he kicked his chair away from him and stormed out of the room.

Phil went back to his desk and spoke to Robert, "Did you find anything?"

"Oh yes," Robert said with a grin. "What the fuck did you do to Cole?"

"Why?" Phil asked. Robert pointed to Murphy's office. Phil looked around and saw Murphy and Cole having a heated argument.

Murphy looked over in Robert and Phil's direction. He got up and walked over to the office window, then he closed the blinds. Robert looked at Phil. "I wonder what's going on there?" Robert asked.

Phil: "I don't know, but I can guess. Anyway what did you find out?"

Robert: "In the past year and a half Grant got regular monthly payments in cash into his account."

"How much?" Phil inquired.

"Almost four hundred thousand dollars all told. I also rolled Cole's finances, by mistake you understand," he said with a grin. "He also got regular payments in cash and guess what it adds up to, almost four hundred thousand. So there's better than a chance that Grant and Cole were on the take and Murphy's a good friend of theirs."

"Do we tell Murphy?"

"No, not yet, I don't want Murphy knowing everything we know, just in case."

"Just in case what?" asked Robert.

"In case he's involved in this. We'll have to talk to Cole again." Phil looked around, "Where is he?"

"He's gone," answered Robert.

Phil: "We'll see him tomorrow morning."

Robert: "Man you've got a real hard one for Murphy."

"Only because that piece of crap has something to do with this. Would you not ask questions if I owned a high class apartment and a big fucking boat? Friend or no friend."

When Cole left the police station it was getting dark as he walked to his car. He suddenly got the feeling that he was being followed, he looked around but there was no one there. He shook his head and laughed quietly to himself.

He got to his car he opened it up and got in then he drove home and parked his car and went to get out. Suddenly a dark figure pounced on him from behind Cole felt a surge of electricity run through his body and then he passed out. The dark figure dragged Cole from his car over to a waiting van and he bundled him into the back.

A short time later Cole came to and found he had been tied down. He tried to look around, but he couldn't see a thing in the very dim room. Suddenly he heard a cackle from the dark and a light appeared overhead. It blinded Cole for a moment. When his eyes adjusted to the bright light he tried to look over to where the cackling was coming from. He saw a figure coming from the dark.

The figure was dressed from head to foot in black, the only thing that wasn't covered was the eyes. The figure then produced a homemade knife and slowly walked over to Cole.

Cole: "Who are you? Do you know who you're fucking with?"

The dark figure put his finger over his lips and whispered "SHHHHH.

Be a good boy now," and brushed his knife down Cole's cheek.

Cole: "Look, don't do anything stupid buddy I'm a cop if you let me go I'll forget all about this I swear, ok?" he said nervously. The figure put his left arm over Cole's chest with the knife in his right hand as he plunged it into his lower abdomen. Cole screamed as the figure slid the knife up into his stomach.

The next morning the phone rang in Phil's apartment. He suddenly opened his eyes and sat up. He got off his bed and slowly walked over to the phone.

Phil: "Hello, what is it?"

Robert: "It's me, partner, come down to the docks. I've got a surprise for you."

Phil got dressed and headed to the docks. Robert spotted him getting out of the car. "Alright, what's the surprise?" asked Phil.

Robert: "Come with me." He escorted Phil to the boat where Grant's body was found the day earlier.

Jack was waiting there. "What's going on?" asked Phil.

Jack pointed in to the boat and said, "He's in there." Phil walked into the boat.

Phil: "Jesus, its Cole. What the fuck happened here?"

Jack: "As you can see, he was cut from the lower abdomen to just past the stomach. Just like Grant except Cole wasn't beaten."

"So it wasn't the same man?" Robert asked.

"Yes it was, he left another calling card, the knife is homemade and very well made. And this." Jack pulled back a piece of plastic sheeting .COLE WAS LIKE BUTTER.

Phil: "What the fuck does that mean?"

Robert had a strange look on his face as he turned to Phil "I've got an idea. I'll see you back at the office."

Murphy walked in, "Holy fuck its Dan what happened?"

"It was the same guy, sir," Phil said.

Phil: "I have to ask you some questions sir."

Murphy asked, "What questions would you have to ask me, McCann."

Phil: "For instance, why were you and Cole arguing yesterday in your office?"

Murphy: "If you must know, the discussion that I and Cole had was about you. He complained about the way his dead partner was being treated and I have to agree with him."

"But sir, the money in their accounts where did they get it. You were their friend you must have suspected something?" asked Phil.

"No, I didn't," Murphy said nervously. "If that's it, go do your job,

McCann."

"Yes, sir, that's it. For now," answered Phil.

Phil headed back to the station. Just as he reached the door to the squad room Robert excitedly shouted to him. Phil walked to his desk, "What is wrong?" he asked Robert.

Robert: "I said I knew where that phrase 'was like butter' came from. I grew up listening to my Uncle Sean's old cop stories. One in particular stuck in my mind. Sean and his buddies got a call about a disturbance. They arrived at the address and kicked in the door. They looked in and saw a man standing in the hallway covered in blood. Sean walked into the living room and he saw a six-year-old boy pointing into the kitchen at his dead mother. All the boy could say was 'mommy'."

Phil: "Ok, as nasty as that case seems, what's it got to do with this case?"

Robert: "The boy's mother was slit from the lower abdomen to the stomach. And look at this," Robert showed Phil the picture of the murder weapon.

Phil: "It's the same knife."

Robert: "It's not the same knife, but a good copy. When they got the kid to the station all he could say was 'the bad man said my mommy was like butter'."

Phil: "What about the sick fuck that they arrested?"

Robert: his name was Paul Moon. His wife was killed two years before hand in a car accident, then his son died soon after of an overdose. It's thought that's why he went off the deep end. They pinned at least eight murders on him and each one of them drug dealers."

Phil: "So the young lad's parents were dealers?"

Robert: "No, Moon made a fuck up, it was the women next door, she was the dealer. The child's father was a doctor and his mother an ordinary house wife. I tried to contact the young boy Joe Lambert but he killed himself ten years ago, he stepped in front of a subway train. And moon died two years ago in a sanatorium."

Phil: "So we have a copy cat on our hands. We had better inform Murphy about this and that Cole and Grant may have been involved in drugs."

A few hours later Murphy walked into the squad room and headed to his office. Robert and Phil went to his office door and knocked. "Come in," roared Murphy. They walked in Murphy asked what they wanted nervously.

"Are you alright captain?" asked Robert.

Murphy: "What do you think? Two of my best friends over the last two days have been murdered so no, I'm not alright? Now what the fuck do you two want?" Robert handed over the report. Murphy asked, "What does this have to do with things?" Murphy started to read then he went to say, "Yes there are a lot of similarities, I admit, but this case was closed in 1971."

Phil: "Yes but we think it maybe a copy cat killer and if you've noticed the reason that Moon said he killed his victims is because they were drug dealers or people that were involved with drug dealers. There is a good chance that Cole and Grant may have been involved in drugs. Maybe that's why they may have been targeted."

Murphy: "Grant and Cole where not involved in anything illegal, they were the two most decorated officers in the precinct. You two try to pin anything like drug dealers onto their good names I will personally end your careers." Murphy angrily threatened. "Now do you two understand? Now get out," Murphy snapped.

Robert and Phil went back to their desk.

Robert: "Murphy was pissed I don't think I've never seen him that agitated before."

Phil: "He was more than agitated, he sounds frightened. Look Robert why don't we go and speak to Cole's wife?"

"Ok let's go," agreed Robert.

They drove to Sara Cole's home, walked to the front door and knocked. They waited for a few moments then the door opened and a small and timid woman stood in the doorway. "Can I help you?" she asked with a quiet voice.

"This is detective McCann and I'm detective Mathews could we come in and ask you a few questions?"

"Yes of course," said Sara.

They followed her into the living room she offered them a seat.

Robert: "My condolences Mrs. Cole but we do have to ask these questions."

Sara interrupted, "Please call me Sara but I was already question by Pat Murphy."

"Captain Murphy?" inquired Phil with a look of suspicion on his face. "What did he ask you?"

Sara: "He asked me whether anybody was hanging around or did anybody call to see Dan. I told him no I never saw or heard anything. But I did notice Pat was nervous when he was questioning me."

"Did your husband have any worries or anybody he was worried about?" asked Phil.

Sara paused for a moment, "Well there was one man whose name is John Dent. He frightened me, he had an evil look about him. Even Dan seemed nervous around him. He came calling for Dan the night before he died and they argued about something. But I have no idea what it was about."

Robert and Phil thanked Sara for her help, left and got into their car

Phil: "Something stinks here that fucker Murphy's involved in this somehow."

Robert: "I don't think so I just think he's afraid of something fucking up his career. He maybe a shithead but that doesn't make him a murderer."

Phil: "You're probably right. Come on let's get back and check up on this guy Dent."

A few hours later Phil walked over to Robert and threw a file on his desk. "Look at that," he said. Robert looked at the file. "This boy Dent must be the luckiest guy in the world."

"It looks like this guy was arrested for drug dealing, attempted murder and assault with a deadly weapon on fifteen different occasions and every time the evidence was lost or witnesses refused to testify."

Phil: "Unfortunately this only proves that someone in the department could have been helping Dent. We know it was Grant and Cole we just don't have any proof. The only time that we can place Cole Grant and Dent together was the first time Dent was arrested. The arresting officers were Cole and Grant."

Robert: "I have no doubt that they were in Dent's pocket, but it doesn't mean that Murphy was involved."

Phil: "Maybe, but Murphy's dirty I know it. Murphy was, by his own admission, close to them. He was either in it with them or he's a fucking moron."

Robert: "Go home, I'll finish up here we'll go and speak to Dent tomorrow and for fuck sake stay out of Murphy's way."

The next morning Phil went to meet Robert at his apartment. "Come on partner, lets go talk to Dent."

They drove to Dent's home. "Nice place," Robert commented.

"I know, he must have sold some cocaine to buy this place," added Phil.

Robert and Phil walked up to the main door and Phil knocked. The door opened and a large well-built and somewhat scary-looking man stood in the doorway. "What do you want?" the man said gruffly. They identified themselves to the man.

Robert: "Mr. John Dent?"

"Yes," the man answered. "I'll ask again, what do you want cop?"

"Did you know two police officers called Grant and Cole?"

Dent: "No, should I know them?"

Phil: "It was reported that a man of your description was seen round Officer Cole's home and your name came up in the investigation."

"What investigation?" asked Dent.

Robert replied, "Did we not say? Grant and Cole were found dead?" Dent looked on in surprise.

Dent: "I didn't do it. I know nothing about it and if you want to ask me any more questions do it through my lawyer." Then he slammed the door.

Robert: "We got a rise out of him, I think he knows something, maybe we should take him in."

Phil: "No, did you see the look of surprise on his face and then the fear. He almost shit himself. We'll give it a little time and come back later. He was the one Cole and Grant were working for, I'd bet my left ball on it."

Later back at the station Robert and Phil were talking when Murphy walked into the squad room. "Mathews and McCann, into my office now," he roared angrily. They walked into the office "I've had an interesting chat with John Dent's lawyer he's threatening to sue the department for harassment of his client. Lay off Dent, that's an order."

Phil: "You do know you're tying our hands on this case, he's a suspect in the murder of two cops and dirty cops at that."

"They were not dirty and you will not bring their names down with unfounded accusations. Now do as I say," ordered Murphy.

Phil stormed out and Robert went after him. "Hold up, Phil, what are you doing?"

"I'm going to have another chat with Dent and this time I'm going to get the truth out of him one way or another," Phil ranted with anger.

Robert: "If you go anywhere near Dent, Murphy will have your balls in a sling. He'll have an excuse to fire you. He doesn't like us, remember?"

Phil: "Well stay here then, I can do this on my own."

Robert: "No, I'll go with you, we're partners after all. If you fuck up your career it's only right I fuck mine up, lets go."

"Thanks partner," Phil said.

A little while later they got to Dent's house. As they got to the door Robert saw that it was ajar. Phil and Robert produced their guns. Robert slowly pushed the door open then walked in and started to carefully search around the house.

They walked into what can only be described as the games room and on the snooker table was the dead body of John Dent. They saw that the body had been left in the same state as the other two and on the wall was written. JOHNNY WAS LIKE BUTTER.

A moment later two uniform cops burst in. "Put the weapons down," the officer ordered. Robert and Phil slowly put their guns down.

Robert: "Officer, look into my inside jacket pocket my I.D's there, we're cops."

The officer reached into Robert's jacket and got his wallet and looked inside. "Detective Mathews?" asked the cop. "Shit, I'm sorry, detective."

Robert: "Don't worry about it. Go call this in, we'll stay here."

A short while later, Jack turned up. "Well boys, what do we have here?" asked Jack.

Robert: "We came to talk to Mr. Dent and found him like that."

Jack: "I would say it's the same person except there's no knife this time he took it with him."

Robert: "Let's go. We can talk to Dent's brother, Richie, his address is in the file as one of his known accomplices."

A short time later they arrived at Richie Dent's apartment Phil knocked on the door of Richie's apartment "Who is it?" came a voice from the other side of the door.

"It's the police, Mr. Dent, we need to ask you some questions can you open the door please?"

Suddenly two loud bangs came from inside the apartment and splinters of wood shot out from the door. Robert and Phil dropped to the ground.

Robert: "The fuck just tried to kill us."

Phil jumped up and kicked the door open. He bolted across the room and caught Dent trying to get out of the window. Phil grabbed him by the hair at the back of his head. He swung him around and threw him to the ground the gun Dent was holding flew to the middle of the floor. Phil put his knee on Dent's neck and pulled his arm up his back dent screamed in pain.

Phil: "Don't be such a baby Richie if you're going to play with guns you have to expect the consequences. Robert throw me over your cuffs." Robert stood there looking terrified and in somewhat of a trance. "Robert snap the fuck out of it and give me your cuffs," roared Phil.

Robert: "Yes, sorry, here," and he throws Phil the cuffs. Phil cuffed Richie and read him his rights as he helped him up and sat him on the chair. "Now be a good boy and sit there quietly." Phil walked over to Robert.

Phil: "You all right partner?"

"Yes, I'm fine, it's ok just a little shaken up the fucker almost killed us," answered Robert.

"We'll have to search this dump you search in there and I'll look out here." Robert went into the bathroom and started to search. He soon noticed the bath panel was loose. He took a small penknife from his pocket and slipped the blade between the panel and the bath. He gave the penknife a little wiggle and the panel popped right off.

Robert looked in under the bath straight away and he spotted a black leather bag. He puts his hand in and pulled out the bag from beneath the bath.

Robert opened the clasp and looked into the bag then he shouted for Phil.

Phil: "Did you find something nice?" Robert showed him the open bag.

"Shit it's like Christmas there's that much snow there. Richie could get the whole block high for a week," Phil joked.

And then he noticed the homemade knife. Phil took a rubber glove from his pocket and lifted the knife from the bag he saw that it had dried blood on it. We have him. They took Richie to the station and booked him in.

Robert and Phil went to the squad room to see the captain they knocked on the office door. Murphy roared, "Come in."

Murphy: "Didn't I warn you two to stay away from John Dent?"

Robert: "It was a coincidence sir we were in the area when we noticed the door was open and we went to investigate. That's what where paid for, isn't it, Captain?"

"Don't be a smart ass Mathews," Murphy replied. "Did you find anything of interest."

Phil: "The homemade knife that was used wasn't at Dent's house we found it at his brother's apartment as well as a large cash of cocaine."

Murphy looked surprised and said with a quiet tone, "Good work, men."

Robert: "The knife has been sent to the lab for tests they should be back in a few hours after that we'll speak to Richie."

Murphy: "I want to watch the interview in the recording room."

A few hours later Jack came in to the squad room and handed the report over to Phil and Robert. "What are you doing here Jack?" asked Phil?

Jack: "Just passing by, I thought you might need this in a hurry. As you can see its Dent's blood and tissue on the knife."

"So, I take it his brother Richie's in the frame."

Phil: "How did you find out about Richie Dent he was only brought in a few hours ago and he was only charged with assault with a deadly weapon and a drugs charge?"

Jack: "Oh, news travels even down to the basement where my little office is."

Robert: "Thanks Jack, it's appreciated. Now we'll go and speak to Dent, I think he's sweated long enough."

They went to the interview suite. Before they went in, Murphy said "Ok, now tread softly we don't want him to clam up."

Robert and Phil walked into the interview room and sat down. Across the table were Richie Dent and his lawyer Mr. Gardner.

Robert: "Well Richie do you care to try to explain the bag of cocaine in your apartment or why you took two shots at us through the door?"

Richie looked at Mr. Gardener, he nodded his head as if to say 'don't answer'.

Dent: "I'll take the fifth on that one," he said with a smug smile on his face.

Phil: "What about the murder of two highly decorated officers and your brother John? Did you want all the drug money for yourself? You got greedy didn't you?" The colour drained from the shocked face of Richie Dent.

Gardener: "This is outrageous. What proof do you have that Mr. Dent has killed anyone?"

Robert: "This is the knife that was used to kill your brother. Similar knives were found next to the bodies of two cops and this one was found in your apartment in the bag with the drugs."

Gardener: "You don't have to answer any more questions."

Richie: "Look, I didn't kill any cops or my brother."

Robert: "Did you know officers Grant or Cole?"

Richie: "Yes I knew them, they were protection."

"They were highly decorated cops why would they fuck up everything for two scumbags like you and your brother?" asked Robert.

"For the money. Johnny was paying them a fortune for protection and anyway who do you think made them highly decorated officers? Us, that's who."

"And how did you do that?" asked Robert.

Richie: "Simple every time someone tried to move in on our turf Johnny called in our protection. They arrested our enemies and got another notch on their belt and a big pay off. But there was somebody else involved, someone bigger than Cole and Grant. I'm not saying anything more I want to cut a deal drop all the charges you have on me and I'll give you the name believe me it'll be worth it."

Phil called the guard, "When he and his lawyer are finished take him back to his cell."

Robert and Phil walked out of the interview room there they meet Murphy. He praised them, "You got him lads, good work."

Phil: "I think he's got a lot more to tell us."

Murphy: "Oh you mean that claptrap about someone more important in a drug ring. It's bullshit he's just trying to buy time."

Robert: "While we have him by the balls we'll let him sweat for tonight and question him again tomorrow. It can't hurt."

Early next morning Phil and Robert headed to the cells. There was a lot of commotion.

Phil: "There's Jack I wonder what he's doing here."

Robert replies, "Lets go find out."

Robert: "Well Jack what's going on here?"

Jack: "Your boy Dent hung himself with his sheets this morning."

Phil: "When did he do it?"

Jack answered, "About a half hour ago, maybe an hour."

"Jesus, how did you get here so fast Jack?" asked Robert.

"I was already here. I had to drop off some documents."

Phil: "We had better go see Murphy."

It only took a few minutes to get to Murphy's office Robert knocked on the door, Murphy beckoned them in with his hand, "What can I do for you?"

Phil: "This case isn't over, someone else was involved and we need to find him, he may have been the killer. There is no way that moron Richie killed anyone I would bank my life on it."

Murphy: "The case is over Richie Dent did it all. Now leave it alone."

Phil: "No, I can't do that captain there are too many loose ends."

Murphy: "You'll do as I say, that's an order, now write up the report."

Phil: "With all due respect, something stinks here, you look very pleased that this case is over, I wonder, maybe you're the man that was in charge."

Murphy: "Excuse me who do you think you're talking to. If you want to have your job by this time tomorrow you'll take that allegation back unless you have proof which I doubt you have," he said with a smile on his face and a smug tone in his voice.

Phil walked over to where the captain was and with a closed fist Phil punched Murphy on the mouth.

Murphy fell to the ground like a sack of bricks. With blood running from his mouth Murphy stood up and said with a hint of satisfaction. "That's all I needed, you're on suspension you son of a bitch now get out." Phil stormed out of the office and Robert went after him.

He caught up with Phil in the garage.

Robert: "What the fuck did you just do? That prick could have you up on charges for this."

Phil: "I know, but that shit has something to do with all this, I'll get the evidence one way or the other." Then he got into the car and drove off.

For the next week Robert was stuck doing paperwork. He tried to get in contact with Phil a dozen times. At the end of his shift he decided to go to Phil's apartment to see how he was doing.

As his shift ended he headed straight to Phil's place. When he got there the door was unlocked so he opened it and walked in. Robert shouted, "It's only me partner, hope you're decent." He suddenly looked down and was horrified to see Phil on the floor dead. Robert examined the body. Phil's face seemed to be burned off and so were his hands. His gut was opened right up to the stomach just like the others but there was nothing written and no knife. There was a ripped and scorched notebook by his corpse. He lifted it and he slipped it into his pocket and called the police.

A while later the lab boys walked in along with Jack.

Jack: "How are you my friend?"

"I'm fine, tell me what you think," asked Robert.

Jack: "Are you sure you want to hear this?"

"Yes," Robert said holding back his grief.

Jack: "The perpetrator knocked him out and cut him from the lower abdomen to the stomach then burnt Phil's face until he was unrecognisable and did the same to his hands. It was all done in a hurry but it looks like the same man, so Dent wasn't guilty, at least not of the murders."

Robert: "But why no knife and no words in blood on the wall something's not right here."

An officer came over to Robert and told him Murphy wanted to see him down at the station right away. He left the apartment and Jack went after him.

Jack: "There was something else, the ashes beside the body, something was lifted." He looked at Robert then smiled, "Well I could be wrong."

Robert: "Thanks Jack, you're a pal."

Robert headed to the precinct and as he walked in Murphy came over to him. "Down to the interview room Mathews, now." They went to the interview room walked in and set down.

Murphy: "Right Mathews, what happened? Get into an argument with Phil you hit him too hard and killed him then you panicked and copied the Dent murders. You left out just enough details to make us think it was someone else. Isn't that right? If you confess now it will go easier on you in the long run."

Robert: "You know, Phil was right, you are an asshole Murphy."

Murphy: "You're the main suspect Mathews so don't fuck with me," he said with an angry yell.

Robert: "No, I'm not, you are Murphy. You're the one Phil knocked on his ass in front of the whole precinct. So go fuck yourself." Robert stood up and walked out.

A few hours later Robert was in his apartment reading the notebook he removed at the crime scene in Phil's apartment. With what he could read he thought to himself, 'Phil suspected Murphy, but this I already knew, and he went to see somebody before he planned to confront Murphy. It could have been this mystery person that killed him. But the only person Phil suspected was Murphy and he was pretty glad when Dent killed himself. That gave Murphy the opportunity to close the case and put the murders on Dent. It looks like it was the captain all along but how do I prove it.?'

Three days later Robert was about to leave for Phil's funeral when Jack turned up at his door half drunk.

Robert: "You alright Jack it looks like you've been celebrating you better come in and sit down before you fall down." Jack sat in the chair and started to cry.

Jack: "The night before Phil was found he came to see me he said he was onto something big, he wanted my help. I was too much of a coward if I had helped him maybe he'd be alive today. I'm sorry Robert but I'm not a brave man. Oh god I think he's after me now, Phil told me everything."

"Jack calm down and tell me what Phil told you."

Jack: "He told me he knew who the killer was he said it was Murphy and that he had proof. Apparently Murphy, Grant and Cole were in it together and Murphy got greedy. He wanted it all for himself so he killed them."

"But why that way?" asked Robert.

"Phil thought because the case was almost 40 years old maybe Murphy thought nobody would remember. He had to make it good and gruesome to scare the Dents. But it didn't so he had to kill Johnny Dent to put Richie in his place."

Robert: "Then he framed Richie so that he would play ball and then Richie wanted to make a deal so he had no other choice but to silence Richie."

Robert sighed, "It makes sense but we have no proof. There's no unusual bank dealings and your word won't be good enough for a court. I've got vacation time owed to me. I'll try to get the proof and if I do I'll confront Murphy I just need a place to do it."

Jack: "I've got a place, it's a small warehouse. I bought it when prices were low. It's run down but it might do." Jack gave Robert the key off his key chain and wrote down the address and handed them to Robert.

Robert: "Stay here Jack, and sleep it off. I'll be back later. Keep the door locked don't answer it for anybody but me. I won't be long." Robert headed to the cemetery for Phil's funeral.

Robert stood at his best friend's graveside. He looked at the casket. He felt his emotions rise and his eyes fill with tears. All he wanted to do was to break down. But he knew he had to stay calm and focused.

After the service Robert looked around at the people that had attended. It looked like half the force was there Phil had a lot of friends and he was well respected in the precinct.

Then Robert spotted Murphy and it seemed at that point as Robert looked at Murphy shaking hands and laughing and joking with the other mourners everything slowed down. Robert clenched his fist all he wanted to do was to walk over to Murphy, take his clenched fist and punch a hole in the centre of his face.

A short time later he walked over to Murphy, the captain put his hand out and Robert begrudgingly took Murphy's hand and requested time off.

Murphy: "Fine, take as long as you want Mathews."

"Thanks captain," replied Robert.

He left and headed back to his apartment. When he got there the door was open. He walked in slowly. "Jack, you here?" Then a shadowy figure came behind Robert and hit him hard. He fell to the floor, rolled around on his back and saw a figure dressed from head to foot in black then passed out.

As he was coming round Robert could hear someone calling his name he opened his eyes and saw two uniformed cops standing over him. Robert stood up, he was uneasy on his feet and staggered over to a chair and sat down and rubbed his head.

He heard a familiar voice coming from the bedroom it was Murphy.

Robert: "What the fuck are you doing in my bed room?"

Murphy: "Why don't you come with me into the bedroom Mathews?"

Robert: "I'm sorry captain, but I'm not that kind of guy I won't walk into a bed room with just anybody."

Murphy: "Get your fucking ass in here now," he said with an irritated tone. Robert got up and entered the bedroom his eyes opened wide with horror. It was Jack, he had been killed just like the others his face like Phil's was unrecognisable.

Murphy: "We have to bring you down town to ask you some questions."

Down at the precinct Robert sat in the interview room trying to go over everything in his head when Murphy entered the room and sat down.

Murphy: "Ok, we got the doc's report, it looks like it is Jack. What happened?"

Robert answered, "How the fuck should I know? I was at the funeral."

"How did he get in to your apartment did he have a key?" asked Murphy.

"No, I let him in before I left," answered Robert.

Murphy: "Then what was he doing there?" Robert got the impression that Murphy was trying to gain information for himself and not for the crime report. He knew he couldn't tell him the truth.

Robert: "Jack was drunk he was upset about Phil. He was in no shape to go to the funeral so I let him sleep it off in my apartment."

"After you got back, what happened?" asked Murphy.

Robert: "Someone hit me from behind before I passed out all I remember seeing was someone dressed in black from head to toe you know the rest."

Murphy: "Ok, you can go. Have you got somewhere to stay?"

Robert: "Don't worry I can go to a motel. Is it all right if I stop at the apartment to get a few things?" Robert asked.

Murphy: "Yes it's alright try not to disturb the scene."

As Robert walked out of the station he thought to himself, now I'm alone I've got no one to turn to I have to do this on my own.

For five days Robert followed Murphy from work to the store to the dry cleaners and then home he thought to himself either Murphy knows I'm onto him or he needs to get a fucking life.

Robert was ready to call it a night when Murphy came running out of his house in a hurry he jumped into his car and drove out of the driveway.

Robert followed him to a private storage depot he stopped his car across the road from the depot and watched Murphy get out of his car. Then he started to talk to the security guard, the guard opened the gate, Murphy got back into his car and drove in.

About 20 minutes later Murphy came back out and waved to the guard as he drove away. Robert waited for a few moments and then stepped out of his car and walked over to the guard station. "Can I help you sir?" asked the guard.

Robert produced his I.D "I'm detective Mathews, I'd like to ask you a couple of questions."

Guard: "Yes detective, certainly, anything I can do to help."

Robert: "What's your name?"

The guard answered "Tom, sir."

Robert: "Ok Tom, the gentleman who just drove away from here."

"Yes, sir, Pat," answered Tom.

"Do you know him well?" asked Robert?

Tom: "He comes here at least once a week always after six p.m."

Robert: "How do you know when he comes here."

Tom: "This book gives all times of arrivals and departures of everybody who comes here."

Robert: "Does he usually come here this late?"

Tom: "No, not as far as I know but then again he wasn't his usual cheery self." Robert thought to himself I've never seen Murphy cheery.

Tom: "He seemed very agitated and nervous."

Robert: "He spoke to you, can you tell me what he said?"

Tom: "Sure, Pat came to the window, he looked very nervous he asked if there was anybody inquiring about him, then he asked if anybody was seen near his shed. I said 'no' and he told me to open the gate, He looked around nervously and got into his car and drove in. But he looked better after he came out."

Robert: "Is there any chance I could see his storage shed?"

Tom: "No, I'm sorry detective, it's more than my job's worth. Robert reached into his pocket and pulled out a hundred dollar note and set it on the counter. He slid the note towards Tom.

Tom looked down and paused for a moment then he grabbed the hundred and slipped it into his pocket. "I never saw you detective. Oh, remember shed 212." Then Tom pushed the button to open the gate.

Robert ran across to his car got in and drove through the gate he soon spotted storage shed 212.

Robert stopped the car and got out. He walked over to the door and tried to open it. The door was locked he took a small cloth pouch from the inside pocket of his jacket he opened the pouch inside it there was a line of tools for picking locks.

Robert proceeded to pick the lock on the shed door a few minutes later he had the door unlocked, he opened the shed door and entered it was dark Robert groped around the wall and eventually found the light switch and turned it on, he looked around.

There was a lot of junk neatly stacked along the walls. Robert looked around and in the corner there was an old chest. He went to open it the lid but it was locked. Robert picked the lock and opened it up and lifted out an old cloth bag and looked inside. To his surprise it was full of cash.

Murphy didn't get this being a captain on the police force he thought to himself. This is why is bank accounts were clean.

There's at least five or six hundred thousand here, he thought as he turned the bag upside down. The bundles of cash fell to the floor and he heard a clanging sound on the ground.

Robert moved the money out of the way, "Mother fucker," he said out loud. It was the missing knife, the one that was used to kill Phil and maybe Jack too.

Robert scooped up the cash and stuffed it back into the cloth bag. He put the lock back on the chest, he turned off the light and closed up the shed and returned to the motel room.

Robert lay on top of the bed wake thinking and then it dawned on him that maybe Murphy wasn't in this thing alone other than Grant and Cole.

This whole thing stinks.

He was sure Murphy was involved but to what extent? Is he working with someone? Did he hire someone to do the killings or did the sick fuck slaughter those people himself? Did Murphy have the balls to slaughter Phil and Jack? I guess I'll found out sooner or later?

The next day Robert woke up early and decided tonight is the night I confront Murphy. He got dressed and took a pen and piece of paper and sat down he started to write a little note to Murphy:

MURPHY
I know what you are and what you've done.
I have proof of your guilt, meet me at the address
on the back of this note at .9:30 pm sharp tonight.
Come alone or the world will know.

Robert folded the note and put it in an envelope sealed it and put Murphy's name on it. Then he drove to the precinct when he walked in to the squad room he noticed that Murphy's secretary wasn't at her desk Robert slipped the note into Murphy's mail.

He then went to one of the store rooms Robert picked up recording equipment and left. Murphy walked into the squad room his secretary handed him his mail then he walked into his office and sat down.

He started to go through his letters he came to a small plain brown envelop there was no address on it just his last name. He opened it a few moments later he looked as if he was in a trance his secretary came into the office Murphy stared at her. "Are you alright captain?" she asked

Murphy: "Yes I'm fine," he showed her the envelope, "who left this?"

Secretary: "I haven't seen that one before it wasn't there when I picked up the mail someone must have slipped it in with the other letters when I was away from my desk sir."

"Ok, cancel all my appointments for the rest of the day," Murphy said to his secretary.

"Yes sir," then she left the office.

Murphy looked at the note again. He scrunched the note up in his hand and stuffed it into his pocket. Then he got up and left the station in a hurry.

Murphy got into his car then drove to his storage shed. He stopped at the security gate and handed over his pass, the guard opened the gate then Murphy drove in.

He stopped at his storage shed, got out of his car and unlocked the door. He walked in and turned on the light before going went over to the chest in the corner. He unlocked it then opened it.

Murphy looked inside. To his surprise the bag that held the money was gone. He closed the chest slowly and thought to himself, I'm fucked. He sat on top of the lid and lent back then took his gun from the holster.

With his hand trembling, he put the barrel of the gun in his mouth and shut his eyes tight as he slowly pulled on the trigger. He heard a loud click and nervously jumped, the gun didn't go off.

Murphy opened his eyes and looked down at the gun, he noticed the safety was still on. He laughed out loud and said, "Can I do nothing right? I forgot the fucking safety was on," he let out a deep sigh and left the storage depot.

Later that night Murphy went to the address on the back of the note. He pulled up to the warehouse and got out of the car. He looked around it seemed quiet.

He walked to the warehouse and turned the handle but the door stuck a bit. He put his shoulder to the door firmly until it came unstuck and he looked in. It was dark.

Murphy walked in nervously he could barely see where he was going. Suddenly the door slammed shut and a bright light shone down on him from the rafters. The light blinded him for a few moments until his eyes got used to the light and then he tried to look around but he couldn't see anything.

"Alright, I'm here, what do you want? Well come on, speak to me."

A low deep voice came from the dark, "Take your gun out and toss it now you piece of shit."

Murphy reached into his jacket and took his gun and threw it across the floor. "Alright, what do you want? Do you know who I am?" asked Murphy with an angry but nervous tone. "I'm a police captain, you stupid fuck."

A few moments later a cloth bag slid across the floor. "Open the bag," said the voice.

Murphy: "I know what's in the bag."

"Open the fucking bag," the voice said angrily.

Murphy opened the bag, "Ok," he said, "so what, you can do nothing. I have friends in high places this shit can be buried so you can go fuck yourself you won't get no pay off's from me."

Murphy grabbed the sack and went to walk to the door when a figure stepped out of the dark.

Murphy: "Mathews, it's you," he said surprisingly and then laughed.

Robert pointed his gun at Murphy, "Stand your ground shit hawk." Murphy kept laughing and turned to walk away Robert fired a shot into the back of Murphy's leg.

Murphy dropped to the ground and gripped onto his leg with his hands he screamed in pain. "Are you crazy Mathews? You fucking shot me!"

cried Murphy.

Phil: "I'll do a lot more than that to you if you don't tell me what I want to know." Robert threw the homemade knife down beside Murphy.

"There's the knife you used to kill Phil and Jack you sick son of a bitch," then Robert pressed the barrel of his gun to Murphy's head.

Murphy: "I didn't fucking kill them. I was helping Dent ok, I couldn't resist the money but I swear I didn't kill them," he said with a frightened tone. "Please don't fucking shoot, please."

Robert: "Then if you didn't do it, you know who did so tell me who your partner is or I swear I'll spread your brains all over this nice clean floor." Suddenly it came to him, "Oh fuck, no, it can't be him. How could I have been so gullible?"

Robert heard a noise behind him. He stood still as a voice came from the darkness, "Drop the weapon." Robert tossed the gun away. "Now pick Murphy up and put him on that gurney." Another light illuminated.

Over by the wall was a steel table with wheels Robert helped Murphy off the ground and brought him to the table and helped him onto it. "Lay down on the gurney, Murphy, and Robert strap him in tight," said the voice.

Murphy: "Who the fuck are you?"

"Be a good boy now and do as you're told," said the voice. Robert proceeded to strap Murphy to the table.

Then a set of cuffs slid across the floor. "There's a chain on the floor beside you put one cuff on the chain and the other on your wrist," the voice said to Robert.

Robert did as the voice told him. "Alright it's done now how's about you coming out here and showing your face you chicken shit fuck." Robert saw a figure coming from the dark he was all dressed in black he walked into the light lifted his arm and pulled off his black hood.

Murphy: "You, no fucking way, you're dead Jack."

Jack: "When did you know, Robert?"

Robert: "Just now. When you said the warehouse you owned was run down. From the outside yes but the inside is spotless and there's a strong smell of disinfectant. You had to go somewhere private to kill Cole and Grant, you had to make them suffer. And what better place than this. I had an idea Murphy wouldn't have had the balls to do what was done. So he ether had a partner. Or the killings were a separate crime. You played me and Phil from the start. Phil must have been getting close he found something that implicated you somewhere along the line and that's why you had to kill Phil."

Jack: "That story you told him about the young boy watching his parents being murdered, he couldn't let it go."

Robert: "So you were the young boy. Phil found out you faked your own death. So who died on the tracks that night?"

Jack: "Just some homeless guy."

Robert: "So you killed Phil and dragged me in to help fake your own death which was easy you could get your own body from the morgue I guess what a John Doe you beat the face to a pulp and switched dental records and prints, smart. Then you give me the key to this place just to get Murphy here. You must have followed Murphy and me everywhere."

Jack: "I had no choice Murphy wasn't as stupid as Grant and Cole any accounts he had were clean. I didn't know where he stashed his ill-gotten gains and proof of his guilt. So I got you involved, you followed him everywhere still no joy so I decided to make an anonymous call to Murphy all I had to say was I know where your money is. Then the greedy fuck bolted out of his driveway.

"When you followed him I followed you. When Murphy was talking to the guard I got into the storage depot and waited for Murphy to find out what he was hiding. When he left, I got into the shed and found where he was hiding the cash then I planted the knife. I was lucky, you almost caught me coming away from the shed."

Robert: "Why did you not just leave the rest to the cops there was enough evidence to send Murphy away for years."

Jack: "Do you know how many poor souls have lain on my slab over drug overdoses or been killed by addicts or dealers? When I found out that people who swore to serve and protect the public are nothing more than dealers themselves someone had to step up to the plate and do something about these scum bags. If I had left Murphy to the cops he would never have gotten what he deserved."

Robert: "That sick shit Moon really fucked you up."

Jack: "I don't think so, he made it possible for me to see how the world works. You see people like me are the heroes, people like Murphy are the villains and I'm making an example of them. Scum like Dent, Cole and Grant need to die. Drugs destroys lives, drugs fucked up my life. If Moon's son hadn't died of drugs none of this would have happened."

Robert: "There's something I can't figure out. How did you get to Richie Dent?"

"I didn't, Murphy did," answered Jack.

"No I fucking didn't," shouted Murphy.

Then Jack picked up the knife and walked over to Murphy and put the knife to Murphy's throat. Ok, I did, I did killed him I got into the cell block without anybody seeing me, I took the sheets and strangled him and made it look like he took his own life. He could have implicated me I couldn't let that happen." Then Murphy broke down and started to cry.

Jack: "I am sorry Robert, I like you, but after I finish with Murphy I'll have to finish you off. I suppose that's the way it goes," then he smiled and turned to Murphy.

Just as Jack raised the knife Robert shouted, "Not so fast Jack." Jack looked around Robert was standing there with the cuffs in one hand and a gun in the other.

Robert: "You should have searched me Jack. I always carry an extra set of keys and a backup piece you do know you shouldn't have killed Phil, that was a big fucking mistake." Then Robert shot Jack twice in the chest.

As Jack fell to his knees he laughed, "I didn't kill Phil," then he died.

Murphy: "You can't prove any of this. You mention a word of this to anyone and I'll have you hung drawn and quartered now get me out of this." Robert released him from the straps. Murphy got up and limped outside to the car and called in backup.

A while later the backup arrived. Murphy, as usual, was taking all the credit. He roared over to Robert. "Mathews get your lazy ass over here and make your statement."

He walked over and said to the officer, "Arrest Captain Murphy for the murder of Richie Dent and taking bribes extortion and anything I can fucking think of later."

Murphy: "Are you crazy Mathews, you have no proof of these charges."

Robert produced a recording devise and played it back. Murphy stood there with his mouth open. When they took him away he was in shock and didn't say a word. Robert sat down and sighed.

A few seconds later he heard a cop shout, "We've got a live one here." Robert hastily walked over to Jack's car. They were taking someone out of the trunk. He went to see who it was.

Robert: "OH HOLY FUCK." He stood there stunned. It was Phil, he knelt down.

Phil opened his eyes and said "You'll not get rid of me that easily partner." And then he smiled.

THE END

DEATH VISITS BLOOD MANOR

In a solicitor's office twelve people sit with anticipation at the reading of the will of James Arthur Rubenstein.

Solicitor: "This is the last will and testament of James Rubenstein. He wishes me to read some of the family's history as he researched it, and thought that this would be helpful to you all.

"This will all become clear at the end of the will reading and please no questions until the reading has been finished and then I will introduce you all to each other.

"The Rubenstein manor lay empty for seventeen years. It has become a place of legend. It was constructed almost two hundred years ago by a man called Jacob Rubenstein.

"The locals called it the blood manor. Since the manor was built it has been a place of cruelty, the stories begin with Jacob; he was said to be a sadist and a worshipper of evil.

"Jacob had many slaves. People wondered why he had so many when he had no crops and no livestock.

"People from the village could hear chanting and screams coming from the manor late at night and strange things started to happen over the next couple of years.

"Livestock was dying, crops were failing. Bodies of slaves were being found horribly mutilated but the villagers were frightened and tried to ignore the strange goings on.

"Then one night a young girl was found to be missing. They all knew where she was and who took her. They decided to go to the manor and they rapped on the door. A gruff loud male voice came from inside, 'Go away you stinking peasants or I will flay the skins from your bodies.' Then he let out a cruel cackle.

"The villagers used a large part of a cut tree as a battering ram to forcibly open the sturdy door.

"After a few tries the door broke open, they stepped into the large entrance hall and then they heard cackling coming from a room opposite the front door beside the large staircase.

"The young girl's father walked towards the door, he opened it slowly and the rest of the men followed.

"The room was dimly lit and all they could see was the shadow of a large overweight man in front of a huge ornamental fireplace. The fire was blazing in the grate.

"Man: 'do you scum know what you've just done? You interrupted a very important ritual. Do you know what I'm going to do to all of you?' He said with an angry loud tone.

"The girl's father asked him where his daughter was.

"Man: 'her soul is being sacrificed to the demons, the demons that will give me eternal life, now leave while you still can.'

"Girl's father: 'give me my daughter now you devil.'

"Man: 'I am not a devil I am Jacob Rubenstein lord of this manor and your master.' he said with a smug and authoritative tone.

"As Rubenstein rambled, two of the village men grabbed him and threw him to the ground. Lying upon the floor behind him was the young girl, she looked like she was in a state of shock and her dress was ripped. They knew she had been raped and beaten.

"One of the men turned up the ornamental oil lamp as far as it would go and it lit the whole room. They noticed that drawn around the girl was a pentagram and cut into her forehead was an inverted cross.

"Her father knelt down and held her in his arms and with tears in his eyes and anger in his voice he ordered the other men to take Rubenstein to the centre of the village and to tie him to a stake.

"He carried his daughter to the elder woman of the village and she examined the young girl.

"Elder woman: 'she will be with child. The child will be cursed and your family and Rubenstein's will be entwined until this curse is broken or both the family lines are ended.'

"The girl's father, at hearing this, cried out loudly in grief, he bolted out of the old woman's house and rushed over to where Rubenstein was bound. He stood with a look of madness in his eyes but Rubenstein looked back at the girl's father and laughed.

"Rubenstein: 'you should be proud she will spawn the coming of the new age. My demon child will have the world at its feet. Even if you kill me you can't stop the demon and I will sit on the right hand of the master and watch the down fall of humanity.'

"The young girl's fathers took a bucket of oil and threw it over Rubenstein then he took a torch and set light to the oil-soaked lord. He lit up like a roman candle screaming for what seemed like forever.

"News travelled fast to Rubenstein's family. They were told what he had done, that the peasant girl was with child and that the villagers would kill the child when it was born as call it a demon child.

"Rubenstein's father could not let this happen even though the child was illegitimate because it was still Rubenstein blood flowing through it's body. To keep his son's indiscretions a secret, he had the village destroyed and the girl taken to a secret location. He had her father killed for his part in his son's death.

"The young girl had died during the birth of the child old Rubenstein raised the child as his own.

"Over the years, blood manor has been inhabited only by Rubenstein's, the last member being James.

"Now down through the years none of the inhabitant have lived past 60 years of age and none of them have died by natural causes. They have all either had horrible accidents, suicides and in some cases murder.

"I know that none of you know each other as the family was not close. So from my left, we'll start with Carl Winslow, next is Julie Carter, Dr. Sharon Morgan and her brother Joe. This is Martin Williams and Alex Page, next Rose Rubenstein, Jock Rubenstein, Gloria Stern, Natasha Pullman, Lee Craven and Ron Holden."

They all greeted each other with a friendly handshakes and smiles.

Solicitor: "I, James Arthur Rubenstein being of sound mind and body bequeath to all of my living relatives my entire fortune."

Alex: "How much is this fortune?"

Solicitor: "His entire estate is in the region of 50 million pounds but there is a stipulation you must all spend four nights in the ancestral home of blood manor."

Sharon: "Joe and I have to return to the city tomorrow, just write us our cheques and we'll be on our way," she said with a smile.

Solicitor: "You must stay in the manor for four days to collect any inheritance and if you're not there you get nothing, There is one more thing, the manor doors and windows have been fitted with special glass and locks."

Lee: "What sort of special glass and locks?"

Solicitor: "The glass is four inches thick and bullet proof and the locks are timed."

Rose: "What does timed mean?"

Solicitor: "When you walk into the manor on Friday morning every door and window will automatically lock and will reopen on Tuesday morning when I will be waiting there with your inheritance."

Carl: "This is outrages, I'm not being locked into an old house for four days with people I don't know." Everybody agreed that this was not an option.

Solicitor: "If one or more of you do not turn up you do not get your share of the inheritance. Your share will be given to the relatives that do spend the allotted time in blood manor. I will hopefully see you all on Friday until then ladies and gentlemen, good day."

Early Friday morning when the solicitor drove up to the old manor he was not surprised to see that all the Rubenstein relatives had turned up.

He stopped his car at the main entrance, took his briefcase from the passenger seat and got out. He walked up to the relatives and opened the case.

Solicitor: "I'm glad to see all of you decided to attend today. Please sign this document, it's just to say that you all have came here today and agree with the terms and conditions of the will." Each of them signed the contract and handed it back to the solicitor.

Solicitor: "Well now that's done you will all proceed into the manor. There is a disk in the DVD player which you must watch before you settle in. There are no phones and no way of contacting the outside world. Now if you please enter the manor."

They started to enter blood manor, and as they did they felt a foreboding.

Ron: "Tell me something how did the old man die anyway."

Solicitor: "James hung himself with a length of barbed wire."

Ron: "Jesus, what a way to go." Then he turned and walked into the manor.

The solicitor looked into the hallway. I'll see you all on Tuesday morning ladies and gentlemen have fun." Then he closed the door.

When the door was shut they could hear the locking mechanism activate and they looked at each other as if to say what do we do next.

Joe: "Maybe it's time we had a look at that DVD." They headed to the living room and sat down in front of the television. Jock turned it on and then pressed play on the DVD. An elderly man appeared on the screen and started to talk.

"I am James Rubenstein and if you're watching this recording I am dead and you are here to fulfil the terms of my will. You have heard some of the legend of blood manor.

"Now I will tell you the rest of the legend which says that the child that was born to Jacob and the young girl he abducted from the village was said to house a particularly nasty demon.

"And that one person from each generation will house the demon until it can find a permanent home someone, it can live in forever.

"Until then it is trapped between worlds, so it has only three choices; find the right body, stay in limbo or end the Rubenstein blood line, kill everybody till there is only one left then all it has to do is wait till the one that it is inhabiting dies a natural death.

"All the Rubensteins that lived in blood manor have come to an untimely death because of suicide, accidents or murder, just as I presume I may have been.

"The reason I gathered you all here is that one of you is infected with the demon one of you killed me and he or she will kill the rest of you unless you find out who it is.

"You are the last of our blood line. If it has found its eternal body it will be venerable while the rest of you live but if not it will kill you to ensure its survival so it can return to where it came from.

"Well that's all I can tell you. Some of you I will see pretty soon, the others, have a wonderful life and I'm sorry but this curse has to end and this is the last chance, so I'll finish by saying goodbye and a sincere good luck."

The television screen went black and they all sat with a dumfounded look on their faces. Julie started to laugh.

Lee: "What the hell is so funny?"

Julie: "Think about it, James is ether crazy or he decided to go out with a laugh, either way on Tuesday we're all very wealthy people."

Natasha: "She's right I'm going to be a millionaire." Then she started to laugh.

Alex: "Well I suppose we should go and see our sleeping accommodation." They all headed to their rooms to clean up.

A while later, in the living room, they were getting to know each other.

Rose: "So Sharon you're a doctor, what hospital do you work in or do you have your own practise?"

Sharon: "I'm not a medical doctor I have a doctorate in history, particularly old structures, castles, estate homes, ancient ruins anything with an old vintage."

Alex: "What about you Joe, are you a doctor too?"

Joe: "No my work is nowhere near as exciting as my sister's. I'm just an investment banker, very boring work but it is somewhat profitable. What do you do?"

Alex: "I was in the army for quite some time but I was invalided out. Now I take work where I can get it."

Rose: "Well I sell cosmetics for a living. Now with this inheritance I could maybe start up my own string of shops. Natasha, what are you going to do with your share?"

Natasha: "I don't know, maybe travel the world and find myself a husband then settle down and have kids."

Ron: "You're not married?"

Natasha: "No I've never had the privilege."

Martin: "Tell me, is anybody here married and have children."

Carl: "I was for a short time but I've never had children."

Martin: "Does no one think that's strange that none of us have any kids?"

Gloria: "It's just a coincidence. It must be nearly time for dinner I'm starving."

Jock: "I take it we have to fend for ourselves. Ok I'll go whip us up something."

An hour or so later they were all talking in the living room when the dinner bell rang and they headed to the dining room. When they got there, to their surprise the dining table was all set out beautifully.

Jock came out of the kitchen with a large trolley full of food. They all sat down to eat.

Sharon: "Oh my god Jock this is marvellous, how did you do this so quickly?" she said with surprise.

Jock: "I worked as a chef in a little high class restaurant in London but I can't take credit, all this was already prepared. The dinner and even the dessert for twelve people for four days including breakfast and supper. It was all packed and frozen."

After they had all finished, Jock asked everyone if they wanted dessert.

Jock: "I found this It's called a black rum chocolate fireball."

Lee: "Why does it have a name like fireball?"

Jock: "Well because you set it alight and it makes a fireball," he said smugly. Then they laughed.

Jock took a match from the matchbox and lit it they all watched with anticipation to see what would happen. Jock put the lighted flame to the dessert. There was a puff and then a flame and everybody clapped and cheered.

Then Jock blew on the flame to put it out, but suddenly the small flame grew and engulfed his head like a flame thrower. He screamed loudly and run into the kitchen.

A shocked Lee ran in after him. He snapped a folded tablecloth from the kitchen table and covered Jock with it as he got him to the ground.

Lee put the fire out and by this time they had all run into the kitchen. Jock had stopped moving and screaming they all stood shocked and quiet.

Lee carefully removed the scorched tablecloth. Julie started to scream when she saw the sight before her.

Jock's face was badly burnt. His skin was slipping off his cheekbone like melting butter off a hot piece of toast.

He struggled for breath then suddenly he just stopped. Lee checked his pulse then with a blank expression on his face he looked around, shook his head and said, "He's gone."

Lee put the tablecloth over Jock's dead body. Then he stood up and walked over to the door where everybody was standing.

Joe: "How the hell did that happen?" he said with a frightened tone.

Alex: "I don't know just a freak accident we're going to have to contact the authorities."

Ron: "We can't remember there is no way out and no phone which means we're stuck."

Rose: "Maybe there's something to this curse," she said nervously, then with a shake in her hand she pointed to where Jock's body was lying.

They all looked around and saw Jock standing with the tablecloth still around his head.

Carl: "I thought you said he was dead, he doesn't look dead to me."

Lee: "He is, I mean he was his pulse was nonexistent."

Jock raised his right hand. He gripped onto the table cloth and slowly pulled it from his head. The cloth fell to the floor and part of Jock's flesh from his face peeled off and hit the ground with sickening splat.

Then he opened his eyes. Martin noticed that his eyes were white and void of any life. Jock then spoke with a strange and terrifying voice.

Jock: "I am going to rip your hearts from your chests and feast on your souls. You are all going to die."

Then he licked what was left of his lips and laughed demonically before he suddenly stopped and looked at each of them saying "Help me please, I hurt, I'm on fire, help." Suddenly his eyeballs started to swell then they burst. A yellow-green substance dripped from his eye sockets down what was left of his face and Jock slumped to the floor.

Lee walked over very carefully to Jock's body. He stooped down to check his pulse, he put his hand over his mouth to try to stop himself from being sick then he put his other hand nervously on Jock's neck, then he stood up.

Lee: "Now he's dead."

Natasha: "That was freaky can someone tell me what just happened?" she said with a panicked tone.

Carl: "We have to store the body, we just can't leave it lying here."

Lee: "Someone else can do it, I checked him twice, my stomach can't take any more."

Ron: "I'll do it but I'll need help, any takers?"

Joe: "I'll help, we'll put him in his bedroom."

Martin: "You'd better make sure you turn the heating off in that room we're here for four days and the last thing we need is the body stinking out the place."

Ron and Joe wrapped Jock's corpse in a sheet and put him on his bed. They turned off the heating and closed the door, then they headed to the living room. When they walked in everything was quiet, they sat down.

Rose: "What now what do we do now? she said calmly.

Lee: "We know there's no way out, so there isn't anything we can do except stay together and at night lock our doors."

Alex: "It's getting late, let's turn in and Lee's right, lock your doors and don't open them for anyone. If there is any truth to the story and with what we've just seen one of us will try and kill the others."

Gloria: "I'm frightened."

Rose: "We all are Gloria, but you have to be brave."

They all bid each other goodnight and retired to their bedrooms. Everybody except Rose fell asleep, she was too frightened. Jock's death was the only thing she could see each time she closed her eyes.

Through most of the night things were quiet, too quiet. Then Rose heard a scratching coming from the other side of her bedroom wall.

The noise was from Joe's room. She put her ear to the wall and the scratching sounds got louder and then it stopped. She heard two voices, one of them was and Joe the other voice she didn't recognise, it sounded strange.

She couldn't make out what was being said until she heard him shout. He seemed to be begging for his life. Rose ran to her bedroom door and opened it, she paused for a moment.

Then she heard a high-pitched scream, she ran to Joe's room and turned the door handle but she found that the room door was locked.

Rose hammered on the door shouting for Joe to open it and for someone to help her. Everybody ran from their rooms towards Joe's room and saw Rose trying to get into his room.

Sharon: "What's going on here? Why are you trying to get into my brother's room?"

Rose: "I heard him scream." Sharon pushed past and knocked on the door.

Sharon: "Come on Joe, open the door Joseph, open the door," she said with a hint of worry in her voice. "There's something wrong."

Alex: "Maybe he's just a heavy sleeper."

Sharon: "No you don't understand, my brother suffers from a sleep disorder any noise at all will waken him up. Please someone open the door."

Alex and Carl rammed the door with their shoulders and it soon opened. Sharon uncontrollably broke down in a flood of tears and screams when she saw what had been done to her brother.

Carl looked at the room. There was blood everywhere, on the walls, on the lampshade, all over the bed. Then he looked at the mirror where the words 'you are all mine' were written in blood.

Martin walked over to Joe's lifeless and mutilated body.

Martin: "Something has ripped into him, the wounds look like a giant cat mauled him, there's bits of his face gone. Its horrible, who could do this to someone?"

Sharon: "You said a cat, he was terrified of cats," she said through her sobbing.

Lee: "It's almost daybreak. There's no point in trying to get to sleep after this we'll lock this room up and everybody get dressed, we'll meet in the sitting room."

A little while later they congregated in the living room. They all sat down, no one spoke and you could feel the fear, which was understandable. Two of them, in the past 24 hours, had been slaughtered.

Rose: "There was someone in the room with Joe, I heard him and someone else talking."

Lee: "Who else did you hear?"

Rose: "I didn't recognise the voice but it sounded strange, different and frightening. When I heard Joe begging for his life, I ran straight to his room when I heard him scream. But there was someone else there, he wasn't alone."

Ron: "You must be mistaken, look the door was locked from the inside, all the windows were locked so if there was someone there how did they get out?"

Rose: "I know what I heard, I didn't imagine it."

Sharon had calmed down and mumbled, "There's only one way in and one way out and the doors locked. It's not impossible."

Natasha: "I understand that you've been through a shock Sharon, but there is no way someone could exit that locked room without being seen."

Sharon: "You don't understand this manor is about two hundred years old."

Lee: "So."

Sharon: "Places like this were built with secret passages and doors anybody that researched or even knew this manor would be able to traverse them."

Ron: "So what you're saying is one of us may be doing this?"

Julie: "Or maybe there is someone else here."

Carl: "What do you mean someone? You do remember what we saw in the kitchen yesterday, I would say it was something that's doing this."

Natasha: "Maybe we should search this place anyway."

Gloria: "Look at Sharon, she's in no condition to go searching anywhere, I could stay with her."

Alex: "I'll stay too, I can search in here the kitchen and the dining room. I suggest you all be careful and stick close together."

While everybody was upstairs searching Alex was in the dining room. He was tapping on the wall to see if there were any hollow spots. He was about to move on when he put his hand on one of the coat hooks, he heard a click and the wall opened up slightly.

He put his hands into the opening and pulled the covering as far as he could. When the light from the window hit the opening, a staircase was revealed. He ran to the hallway and called for the others.

Lee: "What's wrong, have found something?"

He brought them to the dining room and pointed to the hidden staircase.

Natasha: "How did you find that?"

Alex: "I just moved the coat hook and there it was."

Natasha: "How corny it's like something you would see in an old black and white movie, there's no imagination any more," she said with a sarcastic tone.

Ron looked in the kitchen and found a box of candles so he handed one to each of them, then they went to investigate the secret passageway. A while later they had to split up because the passage became passages.

They soon found that each way they went turned out to lead to almost every room in the manor they all soon met in the living room.

Sharon: "What did you find?"

Lee: "There's a passage leading to nearly every room in this place. We searched everywhere but there's no one else here. Whoever is doing this I have a feeling it just maybe one of us."

Sharon: "You're saying that one of us killed my brother and Jock. You did see what happened yesterday in the kitchen or what happened to Joe? No person could do that."

Lee: "I haven't got it all worked out yet but if you think what the old man said on the DVD is the truth you're as crazy as he was. The only thing that's going on here is one of us wants all 50 million for his or herself. There's nothing supernatural going on, its murder plain and simple."

Sharon: "I didn't do it, I couldn't kill anyone let alone my brother," she said loudly and angrily then she stormed out.

Lee: "I didn't mean you particularly I meant it could be any of us."

Natasha: "That was heartless, she just lost her brother have a bit of sympathy," she said with a touch of disgust in her voice.

Carl: "No matter what, we're in trouble whether it is one of us or a so-called demon we have no way out and we have no phones, now what do we do?"

Martin: "We're going to have to make the best of a bad situation. We stay alive until Tuesday then we can get out of here and collect the money. Then the police can take it from there. We watch each other and make sure no one else dies."

A few moments later they heard a scream coming from upstairs. Ron ran out of the open door and then stopped dead, his hand started to shake.

Julie: "What's wrong Ron?"

Sharon appeared at the top of the stairs. She looked terrified. She ran down to the hall and hugged Ron, she started to cry, "I saw it," then she looked up and saw a trickle of blood running from Ron's mouth.

Sharon stood back, Ron's head slid off his shoulders and on to the ground. His head rolled over to Sharon's foot and she looked down in shock and started to scream. She went to run into where the others were standing and they shouted to her to stop but it was too late, she fell to the ground. Rose ran over to where Sharon fell.

Rose: "Oh my god, not her too." She bent down and went to put her hand on Sharon's back but when Sharon got up suddenly, Rose screeched in fear.

Sharon: "I can't do this, I have to get out of here, I can't take any more of this," she exclaimed while panicking.

Rose and Gloria went to comfort her while the rest ducked through the doorway and went to see Ron's body.

Martin: "There's no blood the head and the neck looks like it had been run through with a hot wire just as he ran, through the door."

Alex: "Whatever it was that did this where did it go? Why did the same thing not happen to Sharon when she came through the door?"

Martin took a tall wooden ornament from the table in the hall and waved it in the doorway. "Whatever was used to kill, Ron isn't here now."

Martin, Lee and Carl wrapped Ron up in a sheet and carried him to his bedroom and lay him on the bed.

Lee: "Maybe Sharon was right, maybe there's something to this demon thing."

Martin: "Don't be so bloody ridiculous there's no such thing," he said with an angry tone.

Carl: "Whether it's ridiculous or not, someone or something is killing us off we have to be careful or we'll all end up like them."

Lee: "Ok, let's get down to the others."

When they got to the bottom of the stairs they heard everybody arguing and panicking. Lee roared at the top of his voice, "Will you people shut up we'll never get anywhere with panicking and arguing now sit down." They all sat in their chairs and Lee spoke calmly.

Lee: "Ok we need to find out what's going on and we need to stick together then we might survive this nightmare."

Gloria: "The old man could be right, maybe Jacob did call up something from that ritual all those years ago and it's in one of us."

Natasha: "James Rubenstein was not right in the head, there are no such things as demons he took a legend and blew it out of all proportions. He became obsessed."

Lee: "That's what I was thinking but now I'm not so sure. None of us can explain how Joe, Ron and Jock died. We do know there is no one here except us so if by a stretch of the imagination one of us is possessed by a super natural being we have to find out who and find out quickly."

As it was getting dark, Martin got up and closed the curtains then he turned on the light and suddenly the lights started to flicker wildly.

The room went black and they all sat very still. Then the room started to shake violently and a few moments later they heard an almighty crash. Rose Julie and Natasha screamed in fear.

Then the lights came back on, Gloria looked around and noticed Martin and shrieked. Martin was pinned to the wall with large slivers of glass thrust through his face and chest.

Lee: "Where did all the glass come from? There's nothing broken everything is intact, that's weird."

Sharon: "Now do you believe that this demon is here and its one of us?"

Julie Alex Gloria and Natasha reluctantly agreed.

Rose: "Are you all crazy I admit something strange is going on here but some sort of monster, it's impossible."

Carl: "You said yourself you heard a strange voice coming from Joe's room."

Rose: "That doesn't mean it was a demon, it just means there was another person there. I still think there's someone else here."

Lee: "I agree with Sharon, no matter how ridiculous it may be, there's something here that we can't explain. Just in case we'll have to search the manor again tomorrow when it's bright. Remember keep your doors locked."

Sharon: "Locking the doors didn't stop Joe from being killed," she said with a sarcastic tone.

Lee: "I know but we found the hidden doors in the rooms so we can block them up and maybe get a good night's sleep."

Carl: "It might be a good idea for someone to keep watch while everyone is asleep."

Alex: "That is a good idea I could patrol outside the bedrooms."

Carl: "It's better if two of us were to keep watch I'll stay downstairs and trust me I won't be sleeping," he said with a warning tone in his voice.

The night went through without incident and the next morning Julie slowly edged her way out of the door to her bedroom. She looked over to where Alex was sitting, his chin was buried in his chest and his eyes seemed to be closed.

She called his name, Alex didn't answer. She walked towards Alex and called to him again, there was still no answer. Then she noticed that there was a streak of dried blood down his chin and on his white shirt.

Julie put her hands to her chest and started to scream everybody came running out of their rooms.

Rose looked at Alex and with a nervous sigh she reached over and put her hand on his wrist to check his pulse then Alex jumped up.

Alex: "What are you doing?" he roared with a frightened tone in his voice. When Alex suddenly awoke as he did, he startled them, then they started to laugh.

Alex: "What's everybody laughing at?" he asked with surprise.

Julie: "I saw the blood on your shirt and chin and I thought you were dead." Alex looked at his shirt then he brushed his hand across his nose and smiled shyly and looked at them then sighed.

Alex: "I'm sorry for scaring all of you."

Lee: "It's ok, but what happened to you?"

Alex: "I get nosebleeds, it's what ended my army career. It happens when I'm under great psychological stress, it's nothing I'm proud of. So they gave me a medical discharge."

Natasha: "Where's Carl?"

Sharon: He's probably downstairs asleep, we'd better make sure he's still in one piece," she said jokingly. They all headed to the living room but there was no sign of Carl. Rose and Gloria went to look in the dining room and then they started to scream.

Carl was tied to a chair. His stomach was cut open from side to side and his intestines were oozing from the gaping wound. Thick clots of blood were slowly dripping to the floor. With the look on his lifeless face they were sure that he was still alive while this was being done to him.

At that moment everybody ran to the dining room to see why Gloria and Rose were screaming. When they got there they were shocked and stunned at the sight that was before them. Lee started to be sick.

Alex took the tablecloth from the table and threw it around the blood-soaked body.

Then they walked into the living room they all set down Gloria started to cry.

Lee: "Sharon, you said last night you saw it. What did you see?"

Sharon: "I don't know, I think I saw yellow eyes and a figure at the end of the upstairs landing, I thought it was coming after me. I ran down the stairs but I could have imagined it."

Rose: "What about you Alex?"

Alex: "What about me?" he asked with a surprised tone.

Rose: "We found you with blood on you and when Julie screamed you seemed not to hear her even when she was standing just a few feet away from you. We all heard her and we were in our bedrooms."

Alex: "Look I explained that and as for not hearing Julie scream, I don't know, I'm a heavy sleeper."

Lee: "It doesn't make sense he was with all of us when Jock died and he was there when most of the others died too."

Rose: "What about when Joe was killed, he wasn't with the rest of us. Any one of you could've got into the passageway and killed him."

Lee: "We were all on our own and if you remember, we found you outside Joe's door that night."

Rose: "I didn't kill Joe or the others, how dare you say I had anything to do with this."

Alex: "So it's alright for you to accuse me, but it couldn't possibly be you. You're a hypocrite," he said with an angry tone in his voice.

Sharon: "Incriminations aren't going to do us any good, any one of us could of got to Joe."

Natasha: "Only one of us did, and one of us could have known about the passages but it doesn't explain the rest of the killings."

Julie: "And can anybody explain why we didn't hear anything last night? It looked like Carl was aware when that was done to him.

Gloria: "Yes, I know, his face was frightening. To think he was watching while he was being gutted, it doesn't bear thinking about."

Julie: "Maybe we were drugged."

Sharon: "That's impossible, if that was the case we would feel the after affects like drowsiness or even a hangover-like headache."

Alex: "I thought I heard you say you weren't a medical doctor."

Sharon: "I'm not but my job takes me to remote out of the way places it's always handy to have some medical knowledge just in case."

Lee: "Nonetheless, this is getting us nowhere. There are only seven of us left and we still have two days trapped in this house, it's time we thought of survival."

Alex: "It seems no matter what we do, someone dies. We have to find out who or even what is doing this. I'm personally leaning towards the what," he said sarcastically.

Lee: "What we have to do is search this place from top to bottom just to make sure there's no one here then we can rule out some other person."

Gloria: "Then we'll know it's one of us for definite."

Lee: "We'll split into two teams of four and three. The team with four members will start at the top and the others check this floor and the basement. We'll meet back here in the living room."

It took hours to search the large mansion but when they had finished they met in the living room.

Lee: "Where's Gloria?"

Sharon: "She was with us just a while ago."

They decided to go and look for her but just as they got to the stairs they saw Gloria walking down them. She stopped and looked at each of them.

Gloria: "Ok what's happened now, what's wrong?"

Julie: "You went missing. Where the hell did you disappear to, we were worried?"

Gloria: "I'm sorry I heard something and went to have a look, I told Sharon."

Sharon: "I didn't hear you, I'm sorry."

Alex: "Well, no harm done, did anybody find anything."

Lee: "We found some weapons they look like decent, they must have been part of an old collection. They may come in handy if nothing else we might feel a little safer with something in our hands so that we can defend ourselves."

Gloria: "Weapons didn't do the rest any good, they all still died."

They sat around for the rest of the day till it started to get dark.

Rose: "We need to eat, if a few of you would come with me I could rustle something up."

Natasha: "We should all go but first someone has to get rid of Carl. I don't know about all of you but I don't want to be eating while Carl sits there in the state he's in."

Alex: "Crap, not again," he then took a deep sigh. "Ok, I'll get the sheet will you give me a hand Lee?"

Lee said, "Ok." They took Carl's lifeless body to his room and closed the door. They went back to the kitchen where Rose was cooking up some food. When she had finished they started to eat and talked about what they were going to do next.

When they had finished they all thanked Rose for the meal and as they talked they felt at ease. Then the lights flickered. They all looked at the lights and at each other as they all held their breath with anticipation and fear. The lights stopped flickering just as suddenly as they started.

Each of them took a deep sigh and they started to laugh.

Sharon: "My heart's pounding like jungle drums, I thought something was going to happen."

Just then the lights went out and everything went black. Rose, Gloria and Sharon started to scream.

Lee roared loudly, "Shut up, be quiet, nobody move just stay still." They could hear a scratching on the table like nails on a chalkboard he took a matchbox from his pocket.

He opened it and took a match between his fingers and went to strike it but then he paused just for a second as Jock's death flashed into his mind. He didn't want to go out that way but he had to find out what was making the scratching sounds. He lit the match and then lit the candle that was on the table.

Just as the small flame lit up the room everybody looked in the direction that the scratching was coming from. There they saw Gloria with her head down and her hair covering her face. She wasn't moving, so Sharon got up off her seat and slowly walked over to Gloria with her hands trembling. Sharon shook her and called out her name and asked her if she alright.

Gloria: "Oh I'm fine, are you all right?" Then she wrapped her fingers around Sharon's wrist. Sharon began to scream and Gloria began to laugh. She looked up and her face looked distorted with yellow eyes and blue glowing veins running all over her face.

Gloria stood up and raised Sharon's arm over her head. Sharon's feet were dangling off the ground.

Gloria, still laughing, took her free hand and clenched her fist as she punched Sharon in the centre of her face. Gloria's fist pulverised Sharon's face as half of the back of her head came apart and Gloria's brains splattered all over the room.

Gloria let Sharon's limp body fall to the floor and Lee grabbed one of the swords that he had found. He ran towards her and swung the blade. He hit Gloria on the arm and a yellow-green puss-like substance came squirting from the open wound. She screamed in pain and then she ran towards the living room.

They all grabbed a weapon and bolted after her. When they got to the living room Gloria was standing in front of the large ornate fireplace. She looked at the gash on her arm and then she spoke in a deep and frightening voice.

Gloria: "You will pay for what you have done. You will all die by your friend's hands." Then she spoke what seemed to be some sort of ancient incantation, she threw her arms in the air and vanished in a bright ball of flames.

Rose: "What did she mean we would die by the hands of our friends? We don't have any friends here."

Alex: "She's bluffing she wants all the inheritance for herself and somehow she set us up, this whole thing is one big illusion. Bitch, she's mad, she's out of her mind," he said angrily.

Alex: "Have the money it isn't worth my life," he roared out loud.

Lee: "I doubt it's an illusion. Right we're going to have to find her and..." Just then Lee was interrupted by a noise coming from the bedrooms.

Julie: "It sounded like someone's up there it's her I'm going to kill her," she said with a spark of determination in her voice. She lifted one of the weapons and took a lit candle and they slowly walked up the stairs.

When they got to the top they stood on the landing listening for a noise. They heard a loud bang on Joe's bedroom door.

Julie gave the candle to Natasha.

Julie: "Hold this, I'm going to kill that bitch myself, stay here."

Natasha: "Don't be so stupid Julie, you can't do this on your own."

Julie raised her sword and pointed it at them.

Julie: "I said, stay here, she's mine." She walked to the door and put her hand on the handle of the door then she turned it and swung the door open.

She stood there in shock then she dropped the sword and started to walk backwards she put her back tightly against the wall and screamed.

Alex: "What's wrong Julie?" She couldn't stop screaming Alex run over to her and grabbed her by the shoulders, "What's wrong?" he kept asking.

Natasha: "Alex, Julie, get out of the way," she screamed.

At that moment Alex felt a hand on his shoulder then he could feel himself being thrown across the landing.

When he looked over to see who had thrown him, he was stunned to see who did it.

Alex: "No way, you're dead." It was Joe, he became some sort of living dead he grabbed Julie and with his bare hands slowly ripped her scalp off her head. As she screamed with fright and in pain, Lee and the others rushed over to help Julie and they pushed Joe across the landing.

By the time they stopped the attack Joe had torn half of Julie's face off she was a mess. Alex ran over to her, took off his shirt and pressed it to her wounds as he tried to stop her from bleeding to death. But it was too late, she was already dead. He let out a deep sigh and put his hands over his face, then started to cry.

Alex: "We're not going to get out of here alive, we're all going to die."

Lee noticed that Joe was getting up so he ran over to where he was and started stabbing him. It did no good.

Joe was still getting up so he then swung the edge of the sword down hard on the back of his neck. Joe's head rolled across the landing and his body dropped to the floor it wasn't getting up again. Lee walked over to Rose, Natasha and Alex.

Lee: "It's all over for now, we can set up camp in the living room. Maybe we can come up with some sort of plan, let's go."

As they started to go downstairs, they heard a grunting noise coming from behind them and Natasha looked to see what it was. All the rest of the corpses had become reanimated and started to stumble after them.

They ran downstairs and closed the two sliding doors that separated the hall from the living room and began to barricade themselves in. When they had finished they sat down and rested.

Rose: "Tell me why we locked ourselves in here again, it was pretty stupid. I don't think Gloria needs doors," she said sarcastically

Lee: "I don't think so."

Alex: "And why do you not think so."

Lee: "I think she's weak, that's why she had to get the dead corpses to do her dirty work. She was wounded and I don't think she is fit for a long drawn out fight that's why she needed to kill some of us before she could show her true face."

"I suspect she's not indestructible that's why she couldn't take us all on at once. Now she's thinned out the herd she may decided to try to take the rest of us out all at once."

Alex: "Just like old James said, she's vulnerable while the rest of us are still alive even if she has found the body she can live in for eternity. Lee proved that by hurting her with that sword."

Rose: "So probably if the ritual had been completed when it was started this wouldn't have happened."

Lee: "The way I see it none of us would have been born if the ritual had been completed. I think we're all directly related to that young village girl."

Rose: "So what do we do now, wait here till those zombies burst in and rip us apart?"

Lee: "You're half right, we sit here and wait and hopefully the door will hold, then we make a run for it at eight o'clock Tuesday morning, when we make our move."

Early Tuesday morning came slowly, it was six o'clock and the door was ready to give.

Rose: "We only have two hours to go, to quote a famous tennis player, 'you cannot be serious'," she said with a nervous but sarcastic tone.

Lee: "Remember taking off their heads seems to put them down and it keeps them down, all we have to do is get past them and wait by the front door till eight o'clock and then we get the hell out of here. Suddenly the zombies broke the door and awkwardly hurried towards them.

Lee, Natasha, Rose and Alex headed towards their un-dead relatives with their weapons raised, they looked at each other and started to fight.

A few moments later they heard a scream. Natasha looked around and to her horror she saw Ron and Julie ripping open Rose's chest.

As they started to pull her insides out with blood everywhere, Lee walked over and violently started hacking at Julie and Ron till their bodies stopped moving. Lee kicked away what was left of their bodies and knelt down, Rose was still alive.

Rose: "Don't let me become that bitch's weapon," she said with blood flowing from her mouth and with tears in her eyes. Then she closed her eyes and died.

Alex raised his sword and with one strong swipe it was done, he made sure Rose wouldn't be coming back. They stood at the front door waiting for it to open, it was the longest hour and forty-five minutes of their lives.

Alex: "Only another ten minutes to go," he said with a triumphant grin.

The three of them started to laugh. Lee turned to Alex and smiled. Then he heard a thud and Alex leant back slightly with his face bright red and his eyes bulging from his head. Alex looked down at his stomach as suddenly a hand burst from his gut with a sickening squelch then Alex fell to the ground, dead. Natasha and Lee saw Gloria standing there looking at her blood-soaked hand and she started to laugh.

Gloria: "Only two little skin bags to go, your mine now," she cackled wildly and took a swipe for Lee. As she hit him with her long sharp nails on the ribs, he fell to the ground and hit his head on the wall and knocked himself out.

Natasha stood with her back against the front door trembling with fear.

Gloria: "I have you now I'll see you in hell." Then she smiled a demonic smile. She started to laugh.

Natasha felt the sword in her hand and with a mighty burst of adrenaline she swung the sword. She took Gloria's head clean off her shoulders her body fell to the ground and her head rolled down the hall.

Natasha: "You first bitch," she said with a satisfied tone. Then she heard Lee groaning, he was still alive. She helped him to his feet and took his arm and put it around her shoulder. A few seconds later they heard a loud click. Natasha turned the handle and the door opened and they stepped out. Natasha started to cry and hugged Lee.

A few moments later a flashy black limo drove up the path and out stepped the solicitor. He looked at Natasha and Lee standing there looking tired with dried blood over their clothes and faces. He walked over to them and opened his briefcase. He took two cheques worth 25 million pounds each then he handed Natasha and Lee one apiece.

Solicitor: "Well done, you survived."

Lee: "Who's in the fancy limo?" A man stepped out of it and walked over to them they noticed to their surprise that it was James Rubenstein.

Lee: "You're dead, what's going on?" James had a cheeky smile on his face as he explained.

James: "I faked my own death to get my remaining relatives together in the hope that one of them would destroy this evil curse that our greedy forefather brought upon our family. I didn't fancy dying horribly like the rest that came before us. So I got the idea to get the rest of my family together to end this curse."

Natasha: "What about the bodies? What are you going to do with them?"

James: "The cleanup crew will take care of that. It will be like it never happened. It was the best 50 million I've ever spent, a small price to pay to live without fear."

Lee took his sword and fired it through James chest. He dropped to his knees and then fell forwards. The sword slid slowly through to his back, he grunted and then died.

Lee: "You should have spent a little more because it didn't work, you son of a bitch." They looked at the solicitor as he stood there shaking with fear.

They walked past him and got into the limo. Natasha closed the door, wound down the window, and called to the solicitor.

Natasha: "Hey you tell the cleanup crew to clean that crap off our property." Then they drove away.

THE END

THE CLAWS WIN DEMON

John Crane was an unemployed family man who was in a lot of debt to the wrong people. He sat in his bedroom on the edge of his bed with tears in his eyes. He was at the end of his wits.

He hadn't got the money to pay the loan sharks he owed and he had no way of supporting his family. He grabbed a gun from under his pillow looked at it then thought to himself, 'there's only one way out, I have to kill myself, my wife and kids will be better off without me.'

He put the gun under his chin and pulled the trigger. His wife ran to the bedroom and opened the door. She saw her husband lying on the floor in a pool of his own blood and screamed.

One year later John awoke from a coma. He slowly opened his eyes and looked around. It looked like he was in a hospital ward. There were bars on the windows and the place looked run down.

John thought to himself, 'this is a strange hospital.' He tried to speak as a nurse came rushing over to him.

Nurse: "Ok John, keep calm, don't try to talk. I'll get a doctor," then she ran to the phone.

A short while later a doctor appeared at the foot of his bed. John tried to speak again.

Doctor: "Don't try to talk and don't worry, your voice will return. You'll also feel pretty weak for a time. It's to be expected. You've been in a coma for almost twelve months, Mr. Crane." The doctor checks John's vitals and gives him something to make him sleep.

As John drifts off to sleep he watches the doctor and nurse argue.

The next morning John woke with a dry mouth. He reached to the bedside locker for a glass of water. The nurse saw him struggling and ran over to help him. She put the glass to his lips. John takes a gulp of water from the glass and coughed. The nurse wiped his mouth and smiled. John said, "Thank you," with a sore voice.

A few minutes later the doctor walked onto the ward. "Hello John," he said with a smile. "How are we doing today?"

John: "I'm fine, could you tell me where I am doctor?"

Doctor: "You're in Claw Win Sanatorium."

John: Why am I here? What's wrong with me?"

Doctor: "I was afraid of this, you've lost some memory due to your injury."

John: "What injury? Was I in some sort of accident?"

Doctor: "You tried to take your own life. You put a small calibre pistol under your chin and shot yourself. You were a very lucky man John. Do you remember your family, friends, anything before the shooting?"

John: "I can't remember anything, but I don't understand, I can remember my name my childhood, where I worked, but that's it. I can't remember anything else let alone shooting myself? What's wrong with me doctor?"

Doctor: "Don't worry John with the damage you sustained from the gun shot you're lucky to be awake. There could be a chance you'll regain your memory in time, now lie down and calm yourself. We'll get you a wheelchair and get you up and about later this afternoon. I'll speak to you later."

The doctor left the ward and the nurse looked over at John and smiled at him. Then he dropped back off to sleep.

Over the next few weeks with the help of the physiotherapist John got back on his feet. John asked the doctor why he was the only patient there.

Doctor: "You're not the only patient here, John, you were just the only one in a coma. You'll soon be joining the main population. You'll be put in a dorm with others just like yourself."

John: "What do you mean, people like me?" he enquired.

Doctor: "People with a high risk of suicide if we put all of you in the same dorm ward cuts down our manpower. We only have so much funding to keep this sanatorium open."

John: "Is that why this place is so run down?"

"Yes we have to run this old hospital on a tight budget. It's an experimental treatment you see, we don't use the usual method here," the doctor answered.

"Do you know the history of this place?" asked John.

Doctor: "The sanatorium was opened at the turn of the twentieth century and was shut down over some sort of scandal, I don't know the details. I do know this facility held over 800 inmates until 1963 when they closed it.

"We only use a tenth of the facility at the moment. If everything turns out well the whole facility will be reopened but for now the rest of this place is closed off. At the moment, we have nine other patients and five residential staff including myself."

John: "When do I meet my roommates and the rest of my jailers?"

Doctor: "Please you have to understand because you can't remember why you tried to kill yourself it doesn't mean that you won't try it again. Now we'll be trying you on some experimental drugs starting tonight and tomorrow I'll introduce you to your new – as you called them – roommates."

That night John was awoken by a loud blood-curdling scream. He jumped up from his bed and walked slowly towards the door. He could feel his heart thumping through his chest as he gripped the handle firmly and turned it. When the door swung open John let out a loud scream and fell to the floor in fear.

A shadowy figure walked towards him from the doorway. John couldn't move, he was paralysed with a deep foreboding fear, until the figure stepped into the light and John realised it was the doctor.

Doctor: "John, are you alright? John, snap out of it, look at me."

John: "Doc it's you. What the fuck happened? I heard a scream, what happened? Is everybody alright?" he enquired with an alarmed tone.

Doctor: "Everything's fine John, your nurse went to the staff room to get a cup of coffee the electrics here are old the light bulb blew and she took a fall in the dark and twisted her ankle and also gave herself quite a nasty gash on the head. Now, are you alright?" The doctor helped John off the floor.

John: "I'm fine I feel pretty stupid doc. I'm sorry, I'll be ok," he said with a sigh of relief.

Doctor: "It's ok, don't worry about it, this place sometimes gives even me the willies. Now if you'll be alright I'll go and patch Nurse Watson up. Goodnight John."

John: "Goodnight doc." The doctor left and closed the door behind him. John walked to the wash basin and looked at his reflection. He stared at the scar under his chin. 'Why the fuck did I do it and why can't I remember?' he thought to himself. He got back into bed and soon fell asleep.

The next morning John woke up as the doctor was standing over him.

Doctor: "Are you ready to meet everybody?" he said with a smile on his face.

John: "I'm looking forward to it doc. How's Nurse Watson doing?"

Doctor: "She's doing fine. She's in the staff infirmary with a sprained ankle a mild concussion and seven stitches in her head."

John: "Tell her I was asking after her and I'll see her when she gets better."

Doctor: "Nurse Watson will appreciate it. Now get dressed and we'll go and meet everybody."

A little while later, the doctor brought John to the main common room

60

aria.

Doctor: "This is my office if you need to talk about anything, my door is always open. Over there is the main community area, and this is the kitchen. Here are the bedrooms as you can see they are never locked, and you can walk about or use the kitchen anytime you wish day or night."

John: "Why are the doors never locked? This is an asylum after all."

Doctor: "Many people with suicidal tendencies suffer from sleep disorders and being locked in adds to their anxieties so I had the locks removed. Now let's introduce you to everyone."

The doctor called everyone together and they sat down on the chairs that were placed in a circle.

Doctor: "Ladies and gentlemen, this is John the last member of our merry little band. John, let me introduce you. Starting with the lady on your left. Lily, David, Collin, Sasha, Paul, Thomas, Sean, Liam and last but not least Rebecca. I am Doctor Philips, this is Nurse Ryan, you know Nurse Watson and these two gentlemen are Josh and Peter our orderlies.

"Now that we all know each other's names let's get started. You all have one thing in common, suicide, all of you tried to end your lives."

Collin: "Tell me doctor, why can none of us remember being brought here?"

Liam: "He's right doc, I can remember everything up until a couple of days before I woke up here."

Doctor: "Unfortunately the institutes you were in used typical treatments to dull your senses. When you came here we dried you out and cleaned your systems up. We'll be starting a new experimental drug system and we will be doing group therapy every few days but if you need anything, as I told John, my door is always open. Now Nurse Ryan would like to have a word with you all."

Then Doctor Philips stood up looked around and bid everyone the time of day and he headed for his office.

Nurse Ryan: "Pay attention, these are the rules. You cannot leave these halls. The only ones that have the keys for the main doors to the outside are the doctor, the nurses and the orderlies. There will be under no circumstances, no, I repeat no, sexual contact of any kind. Do I make myself clear? And last but not least, and when you are given your medication you will take it." Then Nurse Ryan walked away to get on with her duties.

John sat in his chair quietly looking at the floor, Sasha sat down beside him, she took him by the hand and shook it.

Sasha: "Hi, I'm Sasha."

"Hello, I'm John," he said nervously.

Sasha: "Did you hear the scream last night? It terrified me."

John: "Yes, it was pretty scary."

David: "I almost shit myself. Then the doc told us what happened, he said this old building makes things sound worse than they are."

Sean: "That's bullshit what we all heard last night was no fucking echo."

John: "What are you trying to say?"

Sean: "I know the history of Claw Win Sanatorium and it's not pretty. It didn't just get shut down over a simple scandal like the doc tells it."

Thomas: "And how the fuck do you know about what happened?"

Sean: "I was brought up around here. When my pop died, mom and me went to stay with my great aunt Mary, she's the one that told me the story when I was young."

Paul: "Ok then, smart ass, what's the story and what's all the mystery about."

Sean: "Claw Win was built in 1902 by a doctor Ryman, he was obsessed with curing mental illness and back then, that was to most doctors an impossibility. This place was a masterpiece, a place to start a new age of psychotherapy. His methods were experimental but they yielded fast results. One of the things that was so different about this sanatorium was that both poor and rich were admitted. Dr Ryman didn't care what you were, or where you came from. For years people held him up as a humanitarian and a great man."

Liam: "Alright we get it, Ryman was a twentieth century Florence Nightingale, so fucking what."

Sean: "Yes but years later people started to notice that the rich folk were coming out but some off the poor folk were never seen again. Eventually government officials raided Claw Win Sanatorium. What they found were horrifying, mutilated people in the basement, the living and dead being experimented on. After what they saw, the officials and the courts had no other recourse but to rule that he was insane and put him in his own asylum. He and his cohorts died here in 1962 or 63. Just after Ryman's death the government shut the place down."

Lily: "What a horrible story is it true?"

Liam: "Of course it isn't, he's just yanking our chains."

Sean: "To be honest I'm not sure Aunt Mary was way out there, but I do know none of us kids would come anywhere near this place day or night."

David: "Well what about now, are you still scared."

Sean: "Yes, this place still scares me shitless, even more so with what we heard last night.

A while later Nurse Ryan came around with the medication on a trolley.

Nurse Ryan: "Everybody come here." Then she stood and made sure that everyone took the pills. She looked at her watch, "It's almost time for bed."

Rebecca: "But it's only five o'clock, Nurse Ryan," she said with a timid voice.

Nurse Ryan: "Yes I know, but the medication will hit your system hard for a few days, so off you go to your rooms," she said sternly.

A few hours later just as John was falling into a peaceful sleep, he heard a quiet knock at his door. He got out of his bed and put his robe on and opened the door. It was Rebecca, she looked startled.

John: "What's wrong Rebecca is everything alright?"

Rebecca: "I was making a cup of coffee when I heard something. It sounded like heavy breathing outside the kitchen door."

John: "Ok come on we'll take a look."

John walked into the common room with Rebecca. There was nobody there. Suddenly a noise came from the kitchen John and Rebecca slowly walked towards the kitchen door when Thomas came through the doorway with a cup of coffee in his hands.

Rebecca screamed and startled Thomas to the extent that he dropped the hot cup of coffee. Rebecca started to cry and then she run to her room. Thomas shouted after her.

Thomas: "It's alright Rebecca don't worry about it."

Everybody came out of their rooms to see what the commotion was about.

Paul: "What the fuck's going on?"

Sasha: "I heard a scream is everyone alright?"

John: "It was Rebecca she came to my room and she said she heard heavy breathing when she was in the kitchen. I came to have a look we heard a noise in the kitchen Thomas came out and scared the crap out of both of us, she started to cry and went to her room.

Collin: "What are you up to Thomas, the old heavy breathing game? Tut, tut you bad boy," he said jokingly.

Thomas: "Fuck yourself it wasn't me I just came out a few seconds before all this."

Liam: "It was probably that story Sean told us, it unnerved all of us. The best thing to do is let her rest and we should do the same thing."

They all headed back to their rooms. A few hours later a loud scream engulfed the quiet halls. John jumped out of his bed and ran to the hall. When he got there everybody was coming out of their rooms.

David: "Jesus what is going on now?"

Sasha: "I heard another scream it sounded like Rebecca."

Collin went to Rebecca's room, "She's not there," he said.

John: "I suggest that we split up and search for her. Lily and David can you go for the doc just in case?"

David: "Ok come on Lily, anything to get a good night's sleep."

The rest went looking for Rebecca.

A few minutes later Thomas, Liam and John heard Sasha calling, "She's here in the bathroom, come quick." They hurried to the bathroom and was greeted with a horrifying sight. Rebecca was lying under the washbasin curled up in a ball and shivering.

Her clothes were splattered with blood and part of the floor was saturated. The doctor walked into the bathroom.

Doctor: "What happened?" he said excitedly as he hurried over to Rebecca. "Are you alright?" The doctor got onto his radio. "Nurse Ryan, Nurse Ryan, are you there? Josh, Peter?"

Josh: "Yes, Sir, Josh here, is there anything wrong?"

Doctor: "Did you see Ryan anywhere?"

Josh: "No, Sir, I haven't seen her for a couple of hours."

Doctor: "Ok look for her and send her to me. Can someone help me carry Rebecca to her room?"

Sean helped the doctor carry her to the bed. They lay her down. Rebecca looked as if she was in a trance.

Doctor: "Where did Ryan go? She was supposed to be here not gallivanting somewhere else."

Lily was cleaning the blood from Rebecca.

Lily: "Doctor, she's not cut."

The doctor looked at Rebecca, "You're right."

"Then where did all the blood come from?" asked Lily.

John: "It's not from any of us, we're all here and none of us seemed to be injured."

Paul: "We're not all here. What about Nurse Ryan? She's missing."

Rebecca: "She's not missing, she's dead. I saw her being ripped apart."

Sean: "If you saw her being killed, then who did it?"

Rebecca: "Not who, but what."

John: "What do you mean, what?"

Rebecca: "It wasn't human, its teeth were like razors and it was strong."

Then she started to cry uncontrollably. The doctor took a small bottle and syringe out of his bag and he gave Rebecca something to make her sleep. When she drifted off the doctor moved everybody to the common room.

Doctor: "She's delusional I doubt she saw anything that she described."

David: "Then you're saying all that blood is in her head too," he said sarcastically.

Doctor: "In rare cases some people can produce a great amount of blood from their own bodies and they don't even realise it's happening. It can happen in times of great stress and the mind makes a horrific vision to protect itself. And in this case I think that's what has happened to Rebecca. It's an amazing phenomenon. I never thought I would see it close up."

John: "Paul's right. Nurse Ryan is still missing and we can't dismiss that something may have happened to her. By the looks of that bathroom, something nasty."

Moments later Josh and Peter walked into the common room.

Doctor: "Well, did you find her?"

Peter: "We've looked everywhere, sir, but we can't find Nurse Ryan anywhere."

Collin: "That proves it. She's dead. We have to call the police." Everybody started to talk over each other.

Doctor: "Calm down everyone," he said with a raised voice. "The truth is Nurse Ryan has an alcohol problem and unfortunately it looks like she fell off the wagon. She'll turn up tomorrow, it's happened before."

Lily: "What about Nurse Watson?"

Doctor: "Nurse Watson is fine, I spoke to her earlier tonight. Hopefully she'll be returning to work tomorrow a little worse for wear but in good spirits. Now I suggest we all try to get some sleep."

"Oh Lily, could you stay with Rebecca tonight and call me if there are any problems."

Lily: "No problem, Doctor Phillips."

The doctor went back to his room.

David: "What the doc said is bullshit, there is no way that what we saw in that bathroom tonight was in anybody's head."

John: "What reason would he have to tell lies?"

Sean: "His reputation this treatment is experimental. If it works he'll be famous in the academic world."

David: "Right, then we should call the cops just to be on the safe side."

Sasha: "And say what? We think there has been a murder, and when they arrive, whose word do you think they'll take? Mad people or the doc's?"

Collin: "She's right, I think we should sleep on it and see what happens tomorrow."

The next morning they all gathered in the common room.

John: "How are you this morning Rebecca? Are you feeling any better?"

Rebecca: "Yes thanks, John, and no I haven't changed my story, I didn't imagine what I saw. I did see Nurse Ryan being killed by something, the only way I can describe it is some sort of demon."

Liam: "Do you realise how crazy that sounds?"

"Yes, I know how it sounds, but I know what I saw," Rebecca said angrily.

Doctor Phillips entered the common room.

Doctor: "I got in touch with Nurse Ryan's family early this morning. I got word back that she's fine and well. It was just like I said, she fell off the wagon."

Rebecca stood up and roared, "I didn't dream this up, I saw what I saw, and nothing can make me think otherwise." She then stormed off down the corridor.

They were all sitting quietly when the orderly Peter burst in. He was in a panic.

Peter: "Doctor, it's Josh, he's dead. I found him in the store room I think he hung himself."

Everybody ran to the storeroom. They saw Josh hanging from a thin piece of wire, when they took a close look at the body they found that Josh had deep rips on his chest and abdomen.

Collin: "I suppose those marks were all in his head, well doc?"

Doctor: "He hung himself, end of story," he said nervously.

John: "Bull, he looks like he's been mauled and where's the blood with those gashes? The place should be covered and if he did kill himself how did he get up there without standing on something?"

Doctor: "Yes, you're right Peter, get the police. Everybody else go back to your rooms and don't touch anything. We must keep everything as we found it."

A few moments later they were standing in the common room when Peter walked in.

Peter: "Sir, the phones are down and I can't open the doors, my key card won't work."

The doctor tried his key card twice but the doors still wouldn't open. "I can't understand it, these things are supposed to be infallible." The doctor told Peter to go and search Josh's body for his key card and then to go to the staff infirmary and bring Nurse Watson to the common room and make sure that she has her key card with her.

David: "What is going on here, doc? We supposedly came here for help and one of the orderlies is found dead and a suspicious death at that. Rebecca is found in a pool of blood that wasn't hers, and there's a nurse missing."

Doctor: "I told you about Nurse Ryan and what may have happened to Rebecca."

Paul: "But can you explain what killed the Josh? That's right, you can't doc."

John: "Either there's someone else here that we don't know about or one of us killed Josh."

Doctor: "Don't be paranoid John there's probably a good explanation for all this." Rebecca came walking towards the common room and John asked how she was. Rebecca said she was ok.

Just at that moment there was a loud scream coming from the staff infirmary.

Doctor: "That sounds like Peter." They all rushed to where the infirmary was there.

They saw Peter being sick in the corridor. After he finished, he pointed towards the door, "In there," he said with a frightened look on his face.

John opened the door slowly and looked in. Over on the bed was Nurse Watson, her chest had been ripped open and there was blood everywhere. He gulped.

Sasha came from behind him and looked in at Nurse Watson's body. She screamed and then fainted. The doctor went to Sasha's aid. She came to a short time later.

Sasha: "It was horrible. Who or what could do something like that to a person?"

John: "I don't know but I'm not sticking around to find out. Peter where are the key cards?"

Peter: "I've got one, I'm not going in there to get the other one. Oh by the way, Doctor Phillips, I quit."

Sean: "It's ok, I'll go get it."

Sean walked into the infirmary and slowly went over to the mutilated corpse he put his hand over his mouth to stop himself from being sick.

As he looked around for the key card he spotted it on the floor in a small pool of thick congealing blood. Sean reached down and begrudgingly picked up the blood-soaked key card and then hurried out into the corridor.

Sean lent against the wall with beads of nervous sweat rolling down his face. He passed the key card to John and said, "I'm never doing that again."

John: "Ok doc, give me the codes." The doctor told John the codes for the main doors.

Everybody headed towards the doors. John tried to use the cards but they didn't work. He tried again but they still didn't work.

John: "What's wrong with these things, doc?"

Doctor: "There shouldn't be anything wrong. It's a new system it was only put in two weeks ago."

Liam ran down the hallway, he got to the common room and grabbed a chair and he hit the window with it. The chair just bounced off and fell to the ground.

Liam: "We need to get out of here," he said in a frightened tone.

Lily: "Calm down, Liam."

Liam: "I'm not staying here to get slaughtered like that, we need to find a way out."

Thomas: "Doctor Phillips, is there any way out of here other than the doors and windows?"

Doctor: "No, Claw Win Sanatorium was built better than a high security prison and that's by today's standards."

John: "Surely if no one hears from us they'll send someone to see if everything alright?"

Doctor: "No they won't, no one knows we're here," he said nervously.

Collin: "I was right that's why we can't remember. You kidnapped us, you drugged us and brought us here, why?"

Doctor: "I and other members of my profession knew that Doctor Ryman's research had merit. We believe that such people as you can be helped."

Sasha: "This is illegal. I'll make sure you and all those who are involved in this will spend the rest of your lives in prison."

Doctor: "You don't understand none of you have been kidnapped. You were all institutionalised by your next of kin they heard of this experimental process and of the experimental medication they signed you all up."

John: "What sort of experiment is this? What's meant to happen and what does the medication do?"

Doctor: "It's all to do with fear. Ryman deduced that fear was a big part of the problem when someone tried to kill themselves, so the plan was to try to induce fear slowly over a period of months and the meds we give you made your fear less worrying and more adept at handling it."

Sean: "But why use fear to combat fear?"

Doctor: "Ryman thought that fear of life can make people end their own lives but fear of being horribly murdered can make the person's mind over ride the self-destructive part of their personality to bring forward self-preservation. We were going to build on the fear. We would start slowly with strange noises, a lot of made up stories and last of all you would find the mutilated bodies of the staff you would be in fear of your own lives towards the end you would see that your lives were a gift not a curse. But the treatment hasn't yet started I don't know what's going on."

Sean: "Then why did Ryman do all those horrible things like turning people into freaks and surgically experimenting on them?"

Doctor: "He took things too far and lost his mind."

Rebecca: "What do we do now?"

John: "We split up into four groups of three and search for a way out. We'll meet back here in the common room when we've finished."

Paul: "Good at least now we've got a plan."

John: "Everybody remember be careful, it's getting late."

It was getting dark and the weather was taking a turn for the worst when they all started to reassemble in the common room.

Thomas: "This place is locked up tighter than a duck's ass, I can't see any way out."

Suddenly the lights started to flicker Sasha and Rebecca started to scream.

Doctor: "Calm down ladies, it's ok, the electrics in this place are old and things like this happens."

Lily: "SHHHH, I can hear something."

Rebecca: "What? I can't hear anything."

Paul: "Wait, she's right, I can hear something too, listen."

Everybody went silent they started to hear a soft low growl which started to get louder. They couldn't distinguish where the sound was coming from until John noticed that Rebecca had a terrified look on her face.

John: "What's wrong Rebecca?" She stretched out her hand and pointed to the area behind the orderly, Peter. John could see through the flickering lights a hunched figure with burning red eyes, and long claw-like fingernails.

John: "Peter, walk very slowly towards us."

Peter: "Why? What's wrong?"

John: "Just do it and don't look behind you, do it now," he said with a calm but nervous tone.

Peter immediately looked behind him and the strange figure opened its mouth and showed two rows of razor-sharp teeth. It let out an unholy screech and pounced on Peter. It viciously started to rip into Peter's body as he screamed with a high pitched voice, "Help me. It's fucking killing me, help!"

Everybody started to scream and they backed up to the far corner of the room where they watched in horror as the strange figure sunk its razor-like teeth into Peter's throat and then it bit a large portion of flesh out of his neck.

While chewing on the large chunk of flesh it started to cackle loudly and before their eyes the human-like beast outstretched its arms and let out a large loud roar and disappeared. They all stood stunned and terrified at what they witnessed.

Doctor: "Peter's still alive." The doctor bolted over to Peter and took his coat off and pressed it against the wound on his throat. Peter looked at the doctor then he closed his eyes and died.

John: "What the fuck was that? Doc, what was that?"

Rebecca: "I told you I wasn't imagining it."

Doctor: "I've never seen anything like that before."

Liam: "What do we do now? We can't get out, we have no weapons so now what?"

David: "The first thing we should do is store these bodies then look for some weapons, and find a place where we can barricade ourselves in for the night."

Doctor: "You're right, but we all need to stick together no one go anywhere alone."

They broke up in two groups, one group put the three bodies in the deep freeze. The second group went to look for weapons. Half an hour later, Lily got separated from the group.

David: "Did anyone see were Lily went?" David called for her, there was no answer. He called for her again. Then they heard her scream. They ran towards. The scream they came to a door and opened it. Lily stood there with her eyes wide open and tears flowing down her face.

David: "There you are, you scared the crap out of me what happened did you get lost?"

Lily: "Help me," she said with a quiet and frightened voice. Then she dropped to her knees. Sasha put her arms around Lily.

Sasha: "What's wrong Lily?" She noticed that Lily's back was all wet and as she took her hand away it was covered with blood. Lily slumped forward Sasha saw four deep rips in her back. She started to scream.

David: "Quick, we have to get her back to the common room."

Back at the common room John and the rest of the group were looking for weapons.

John: "Jesus doc, is this all there is? A few sticks of wood a couple of screwdrivers and two small hammers. There's nothing but plastic knives and forks, what's with that?"

Doctor: "It's an asylum, John, there are no weapons and nothing sharp so no one can hurt themselves."

Sean: "I don't think this lot is going to get the job done somehow."

Rebecca: "I agree, we all saw what that thing has done to Peter and not to mention Nurse Watson and Josh and maybe Nurse Ryan, we have no chance with what we have here."

Liam: "Look Rebecca, don't be so negative, if we think that way none of us will survive. The weapons we've got will just have to do."

Moments later the others were carrying Lily up the corridor David shouted for help. John and the doctor ran to help. They took Lily to the couch.

Doctor: "What happened?"

Sasha: "We noticed she was missing, David called for her, then we heard a scream, we found her like this."

David: "Is she going to be all right doc?"

Doctor: "I don't know, she's lost a lot of blood. This is vicious she wasn't just cut she was ripped open." The doctor bandaged Lily's wounds and gave her a sedative.

Doctor: "That's the best I can do at the moment."

They started to barricade themselves in. When the lights started to flicker they stopped everything and suddenly it went quiet. They looked at each other with anticipation to see what would happen next. Then through the flickering light they saw the hunched figure appear again. It looked at them with those red demonic eyes.

David panicked and lifted one of the screwdrivers from the floor and fired it at the hunched figure. It caught the screwdriver and looked at it then it looked back and with lightening speed the deformed creature threw it back in John's direction. John moved his head and the screwdriver just missed him.

Then the creature pounced forward, grabbed Lily by the hair and dragged her off the couch. It dragged her to the far end of the common room.

While everybody watched, the creature lifted Lily and put both claw-like hands on each side of her throat then it let out a loud cackle.

The creature ripped at her throat slowly and forcefully with what looked like a smile on its face. Lily's throat came apart like an over-ripe tomato the blood squirted and then poured from her neck then she fell to the ground dead.

The creature outstretched its arms and seemed to laugh. It looked at the freshly torn flesh in its claw-like hands and sniffed it.

David lifted a large piece of wood and ran towards the creature with a roar. He hit the hunched creature on the side of the head and it let out a high-pitched scream.

David took another swing with the piece of wood but the creature caught it in mid air and hit David in the chest with its forearm. David flew into the air and hit the wall.

The creature let out a loud growl then looked down at Lily's corpse, grabbed her by the ankle and dragged her away.

John and the doctor ran over to where David was lying. The doctor examined him.

David: "Shit doc, take it easy, that hurts."

Doctor: "You'll be fine, it's a couple of broken ribs. You'll be sore for a while, but I'll give you something for the pain."

John: "That's another one gone doc, there's only ten left now," he said with a worried tone.

Paul: "No, only nine left." John and the doctor looked around and sitting on the chair was Collin with a screwdriver through his eye.

Sasha: "Oh my good god, we're all going to die here," then she started to cry.

Early the next morning they decided to take another look around, maybe there was something they missed last time.

John: "This time we all stick together no one wanders off."

Sasha: "We should be all right. It only attacked at night."

Sean: "I agree with John we can't take any chances we have to be careful."

Rebecca: "I may have a better idea."

Liam: "OH and that would be what."

Rebecca: "Look over there smart ass the blood it left a trail, if we follow the blood we may find a way out."

Liam: "Or we may run into that fucking thing and we might all die at once."

John: "She may be right it must have come in from the outside, so there's a chance if we follow the trail of blood we might find the way out."

Thomas: "That isn't a thing, it's a fucking ghost."

David: "That was no ghost. I hit that thing hard last night and I know I hurt it. It may be strong but it feels pain so it's flesh and blood. That means it's not infallible."

John: "So are we agreed?" They all nodded their heads, yes. "Ok then let's do it."

They followed the blood trail down to the bottom of the corridor the trail stopped at a storeroom. Sean put his hand on the door handle everybody got ready with their makeshift weapons. Sean swung open the door and jumped back. To their relief the creature was nowhere to be seen.

John: "There's nothing in there, it's empty."

Sean: "Turn on the light." When the light was turned on Sean looked in there he saw a congealed pool of blood and Lily's torn blood-stained clothes.

Thomas: "The trail ends here. What do we do now? Wait till it comes back and kills another one of us," he said angrily. The doctor looked up to the ceiling and saw a blood stain.

Doctor: "Look up there. That's where it's gone."

Sasha: "Someone has to have a look."

John: "Give me a boost up, I'll have a look."

The doctor and David gave John a boost, he opened the trap door and looked into the crawl space. He couldn't see very much but he could feel fresh air. John jumped down.

John: "I can't see very much but it looks clear I can feel fresh air. So there could be a way out."

Paul: "That's not telling us much, it's probably the air conditioning."

John: "I know, that's why we're going to have to find a torch so I can go take a look."

Doctor: "You're not going, I am, I got you all into this so I'm going."

John: "Ok doc, do you know where we can get a torch?" The doctor reached into his pocket and produced a small examination torch.

John: "Doc, be careful up there, and remember if you see anything out of the ordinary get your ass back here." David and John helped him through the trap door. He got almost all the way in when he started to scream in pain. The doctor was shouting for someone to help him back. His legs kicked so hard that John and David where knocked to the ground.

Then the doctor's legs went still and limp. The rest of him was slowly dragged through the trap door. Everybody ran towards the common room while John and David closed and barricaded the storeroom door. After that was done they headed back to the others.

When they got back to the common room John and David were confused at what they, saw everybody was beating on the far wall.

David: "What the fuck are you people doing?"

Paul: "Come over here and lend us a hand. We found a door under the plaster."

John: "How did you find it?"

Liam: "Thomas threw a chair against the wall in bad temper and the plaster came off. Then we saw part of a doorframe.

Paul: "Are you three going to talk all day or are you going to help?"

They soon got the hidden door uncovered. Rebecca reached for the handle and turned it, the door wouldn't open. "Its locked," she said with a disappointed tone in her voice.

Sean: "You know, you give up to easy." Then he took his foot and kicked the locked door open. When the dust cleared David took a lighter from his pocket, lit it, and walked in to the hidden room. He spied the light switch he turned it on. The light bulb flickered a little but it still worked. They looked around and saw it was some kind of office.

John lifted the nameplate off the desk and rubbed the dust off it. To his surprise the name on the plate said Dr. Ryman.

John: "Shit, look, this office belonged to Ryman," then he showed them the name plate.

Liam: "So fucking what? It still doesn't get us any closer to getting out of here," he said with an angry tone, and then stormed out.

John: "He's wrong, we may be able to find out what this thing is. We just need to look at his papers and anything else we can get our hands on."

Paul: "This is a waste of time, Ryman died in 1963."

John: "I know but the people he experimented on, may be they weren't all found. You hear about things like this maybe some of them escaped and their offspring came back for revenge."

Sasha: "Jesus, John, this isn't a second rate movie, its real life and we're fighting for our lives here so stop the bullshit," she said angrily.

Later that night while everybody slept, John read everything in the office but he couldn't find much. He searched through the drawers of the old desk. Stuffed at the back of one of the drawers seemed to be some sort of book. It was tightly wedged and it took a few minutes but he got it free.

John opened the book and started to read it. He soon realised it was the private diary of Dr. Ryman. When he finished reading the diary he heard a noise.

He slowly got up from the desk and edged himself to the doorway. He stepped into the common room and turned on the main light and saw that the creature had wrapped a thin piece of wire around David's neck and it was dragging him away. John could see David's eyes bulging from the sockets and his tongue was swollen and blue. John started to shout for everyone to get up, then he reached for a steel lamp and went after the creature. When he turned the corner into the main corridor the creature was gone but to his horror it left David strung up to the light.

As John looked on the rest of the group came around the corner and saw what the creature had done. Sasha and Rebecca started to scream and cry.

Paul, Thomas and Sean helped Rebecca and Sasha back to the common room. John was transfixed on David's body, Liam put his hand on John's shoulder and said, "Come on, let's get back." When they got to the common room everybody was panicking.

Rebecca: "What did you do with David?"

Liam: "We didn't do anything with him."

Rebecca: "You just left him hanging there? Why did you not cut him down?" she roared.

Liam: "We had no other choice you stupid fucker. What were we supposed to do, cut him down and in the meantime that animal comes back for seconds?"

Sasha: "Quit it, this isn't the time for this shit."

John: "I found this jammed at the back of the drawer in the desk. Its Ryman's diary."

Thomas: "So what use is that? Can it get us out of here or help us kill that thing?"

John: "No, but it tells us why this is happening. It gives us insight."

Thomas: "Bullshit, fuck this I'm not sitting around on my ass so that thing can carve me up like a Christmas turkey you all can lie down and die but I'm not going out like that if I have to die I'm going out fighting. Then he lifted a screwdriver and went to walk away.

Sean: "If you go out there on your own you'll die."

Thomas: "If I stay here I'll die anyway. I'm going out my way." Then he walked away.

Liam: "We have to go after him."

John: "It's his choice if we go after him we could all die."

They all sat quietly and looked at each other, the silence was deafening.

Paul: "Alright John, what's so god dammed important about the diary?"

John: "Sean, you said that Dr. Ryman was insane because he experimented on all those people and was obsessed with a cure for mental illness and that he built this place himself."

Sean: "That's the way my aunt told the story."

John: "The true story was that Ryman didn't build Claw Win the army did. They set it up as a private sanatorium with rich clients and everything. It was just a cover but they needed lab rats. They couldn't use the rich, that would have drawn too much unwanted attention, but by admitting the poor for nothing and reportedly giving them the same treatment it hailed Ryman as a humanitarian so people left him alone and he got his lab rats."

Sasha: "Why would the army bank roll Ryman and why would they want to cure mental illness?"

John: "They didn't. Ryman was there to study fear, particularly fear in combat situations. It looked like an early form of a super soldier programme."

Rebecca: "So he was experimenting on people to make fearless solders?"

John: "As the years went on the army ordered Ryman to do more aggressive experiments. By this time the first world war was long over and the army was getting impatient and wanted big results so Ryman soon came up with building a super soldier from scratch.

"He did it, he fucked with their DNA and grew eight what must have been these creatures. He called them specimens but before the second world war started people noticed there was something wrong here and then questions were being asked.

"The army then pulled the plug and used Ryman as a scapegoat then locked him up in his own asylum. Before they scrapped the project, Ryman wrote down his fears that they would destroy his life's work if they did destroy the specimens they missed one out the one that's after us now."

Paul: "How the fuck did it survive all these years without being seen and why start to kill now? Why pick on us? We haven't done anything to it."

John: "I don't have a clue. It's what the thing was bred for, survival. As for why us, this place has been empty for decades, it's an animal, we've impinged on its territory. Its protecting itself but with the human factor built in the thing seems to be enjoying itself."

Liam: "So we're fucked."

John: "No we're not, we fight back. We take a page out of Thomas's book and we go after it but we have to stick together. I doubt that thing will be back tonight, we'll get some sleep and start tomorrow and we'll look for Thomas then we'll kill this fucking thing"

Next morning John woke up, he rubbed his eyes and looked around. He noticed that Rebecca was missing and he woke everybody up.

Sasha: "Is it morning already?" she said through a yawn.

John: "Everybody get up, Rebecca's gone, she must have waited till we went to sleep and left."

Liam: "She must be out trying to find Thomas."

Sasha: "Stupid bitch, what did she think she was doing? Now we're down another one."

Then they heard footsteps coming down the corridor.

Sean: "Quick get into cover." They waited with their weapons clenched tightly in their hands nervously while the footsteps became louder and louder.

"Fuck this," John said, and rushed to the corridor with his weapon raised above his head. As he got to the corner Rebecca appeared with a bag of food she shrieked with fear when she saw John and dropped the bag.

John: "What are you doing?"

Rebecca: "I just thought everybody would like some breakfast she said with a frightened voice.

They all started to laugh with relief that Rebecca was alright. John lifted the bag of food up for her.

John: "Thanks Rebecca, come on let's go eat."

Rebecca smiled then suddenly she let out a loud grunt and her eyes opened wide then there was a spray of blood that hit John in the face. Rebecca stood there trying to talk with blood dripping from her nose and mouth, she fell to her knees and then face down onto the floor.

Standing behind her was the creature holding half of Rebecca's insides in its claws. It looked at them then screeched loudly. Paul grabbed the still stunned John and shouted, "Snap out of it and fucking run."

They ran back to the common room and Sean looked around.

Sean: "It's ok the thing isn't following us."

Everyone stopped and waited.

Then the creature bolted around the corner as fast as a bullet and headed straight for Sean. He tried to run but the creature leaped into the air and swiped with its claws cutting through his neck like a hot knife going through butter. Sean's head rolled off his shoulders and on to the ground.

John, Sasha and Liam run into the old office and closed the broken door. Liam put his back to the door while John and Sasha pulled the desk over to the door. As they wedged the desk tightly against the broken door they could hear the creature making horrible sounds and moving about.

Sasha: "What are we going to do now?"

Liam: "We wait and see what happens."

Sasha: "That's all we've been doing," she said angrily.

John: "We have to get out of here. We'll wait till tonight then we go through that trap door in the store room ceiling."

Sasha: "We tried that before and the doc died remember?" she said sarcastically.

John: "Nonetheless as soon as it's clear we move, ok." They nodded their heads in agreement.

Sasha: "Ok," she said nervously, "but what are we going to do for light?"

John: "We're just going to have to group around till we find our way out.!

A few hours later Liam was listening at the door.

Liam: "I think it's gone. I can't hear anything, it sounds as if it's all clear, I think now would be a good time."

John: "Ok, remember be quiet, keep your head down and whatever you do, even if you see this thing don't panic, now let's go."

They slowly and quietly removed the desk away from the door. John edged his head out of the door and looked around, he snuck out.

John: "Come on, the coast is clear," he said with a whisper.

They slowly and carefully made their way to the storeroom. Liam opened it carefully and they went in. Sasha turned on the light, she looked around.

Sasha. "Do you notice something?"

John: "Notice what?"

Sasha: "No blood and Lily's clothes there gone."

Liam: "Come to think of it, David's body's gone, no blood, no nothing."

John: "To be honest, at this point I don't care, all I want to do is get out of here so are you coming or not?"

They got themselves into the hatchway and started to walk towards the breeze. They came to a grill with a large fan behind it but they could see the outside.

Sasha: "It's the way out," she said with a quiet excitement.

Liam: "Even if we get the grill off, how do we get through the fan?"

John: "We'll get the grill off, then we'll worry about getting through the fan. Right let's get that grill off."

He took the screwdriver and with great difficulty he eventually got all the screws out.

John: "Give me a hand lifting this thing down." Liam and Sasha helped him lift the grill off the wall and they set it quietly down.

Liam: "Any ideas how we stop the fan?"

They suddenly heard a low deep growl they looked in the direction of where it was coming from. They saw the burning red eyes.

John: "This is it, get ready to bash it's head in."

They stood looking at the creature then it jumped from the darkness and with its claw cut Liam's face to shreds. Liam swung around John and Sasha saw that half his face had been ripped off. He fell to the ground dead.

Sasha screamed with fright as the creature ran over. It pushed John onto the floor and ripped Sasha's throat out she fell to the ground the creature bit into her face with its razor sharp teeth and started mauling her.

John stood up and looked at what the creature was doing. It stopped and looked at John and gave him a cruel smile. Then it went on mauling Sasha's corpse.

John knew that the creature didn't see him as a threat. Then he noticed the fan. He decided at that moment that he wasn't going to get out of this alive so he decided that if he had to die then he would take the creature with him.

John: "Hey shithead," he said with a loud and determined tone. The creature looked at John.

John fired the screwdriver and it hit the creature in the eye it screamed in pain and staggered back towards the fan. John saw his chance, he took a run at the creature and grabbed it then he jumped into the large fan. As the blades cut through their flesh their screams could be heard all over the facility.

At the break of dawn a car stopped outside the sanatorium's main entrance. An army colonel got out and used a key card on the door. The door unlocked and as he walked in a voice came from the dark corridor.

"Good morning, Colonel, the test has been completed, the subjects are all gone, it was a success." Suddenly someone grabbed the colonel by the neck and held a screwdriver at the base of his skull.

Colonel: "Alright friend, calm down." He grabbed the colonel's gun and pushed him onto the floor. Then he walked into the light, it was Thomas.

Thomas: "Right fuck head, step into the light." He watched as a man stepped into the light.

Thomas: "Doc Phillips," he said with a surprised tone. "But you're dead, that creature got you, it pulled you through the trap door."

Doctor: "There was no creature it was all in your heads."

Thomas: "But I heard what John said before I went on my own, I stood around the corner and listened. Ryman grew eight specimens one of the last things I heard was that he was afraid the army would destroy them but it looks like you didn't and years later you sick fucks use us as guinea pigs."

Colonel: "I guess you have the right to know," he said smugly. "The doctor here is Ryman's grandson, he came to us with documents that his grandfather hid in the family home. Doctor Philips wanted to carry on his work. You see our country needs an edge, our enemies want to destroy us so we have to hit them first."

Thomas: "So you're going to let these monsters out on an innocent population."

Colonel: "There are no monster's son. Ryman's experiments were on fear and how we can control it; how we can use it to our advantage. He was creating a form of virus in gas form but it was a special compound. It was something we could control as you witnessed. We tell you what you see, like mass hypnoses and whatever group is exposed to the gas kills themselves and they don't even know it. It's a fantastic weapon."

Thomas: "But I saw them being slaughtered."

Doctor: "You haven't been listening, you see what we want you to see, What it means is we can control your fears," he said smugly. Thomas raised the gun and pointed it at them.

Colonel: "Give me the gun son you know you're not going to use it."

Doctor: "The colonel's right. You where picked because the only one you were violent with was yourself. Now put the fucking gun down."

Thomas: "It looks like you don't know me as well as you think doc." He pointed the gun at the colonel and pulled the trigger, the colonel fell to the floor dead. The doctor begged Thomas not to shoot him.

Thomas dropped the gun to the floor and looked at it then he lifted his head, his eyes were glowing red. When he smiled there appeared a mouthful of razor-sharp teeth. He then cackled wildly and in a deep voice said "Run doc, run for your life."

All that could be heard from the asylum that night was blood-curdling screams and horrible demonic laughter.

THE END

THE DEVIL'S DOMAIN

For years people have been looking for evidence of an afterlife proof, that when we die there's a life after death. The investigations have taken place in so called haunted houses and ancient castles. One of the most famous places is the Bermuda Triangle. People called it a doorway to another world and others called it Hell. Years of study have gone into finding the reason for all the strange happenings in that region. Nothing has come out of it but a wide range of guesses.

Harry Zelman at one time was one of these people. He worked tirelessly seeking for answers to the one and only question that was on their minds, do we cease to exist after life or is there something else waiting for us?

Harry came to the conclusion that there isn't anything out there, we're born, we live and we die. He became convinced that that was it. He had worked for a paranormal organisation for several years looking for proof of life after death or a doorway to another world, maybe a better world he visited hundreds of reported haunted spots and so-called spirit doors all over the world but each time he found nothing.

After seven years of travelling the world and finding no evidence of a haunting, he became disillusioned. Even if he had seen something anything with his own eyes he would have been a happier man. He came to the conclusion that the last few years were a waste of time.

He planned on giving up his paranormal studies when his old professor, a Jason Carter, contacted him out of the blue. He arranged a meeting with Harry at his office for the next day.

Harry hadn't spoken to or seen Professor Carter for three years. They had fallen out over a simple disagreement a few years back. That made him wonder what he wanted. Carter wasn't known as a person to forgive or forget but even though they had fallen out, Harry found it comforting to hear the voice of his old mentor again.

The next day Harry drove to Hudson College to see Professor Carter. He arrived at the professor's office and Harry stood there looking at the door. He was nervous to see Carter again, it was the first time since they had fallen out and he didn't know what to expect.

As Harry knocked on the frosted glass the office door swung open and there stood Professor Carter. Harry looked at him and he thought to himself that Carter didn't look well, he looked very pale and withdrawn.

The professor roared out with joy and threw his arms around Harry.

Carter: "It's so good to see you my boy. What's wrong? You look as if you've seen a ghost." Then he let out a hearty laugh.

Harry: "No, I'm fine professor, it's just the last time we spoke we didn't part on good terms."

Carter: "Yes, I know, I'm sorry about that Harry, I was wrong you were right," he said with a deep sigh. "I should have said I was sorry back then, but I'm saying it now. Can you forgive a stupid and hard headed old man?"

Harry: "Of course I can, my old friend, so why did you want to see me so urgently professor."

Carter: "I think we found a smaller version of the Bermuda triangle."

Harry: "Where?" he enquired.

Carter: "In the middle of the Pacific," he said as he pointed to a small area on a map that was lying on his desk.

Harry: "How did you come to this conclusion? There haven't been any reported disappearances in that area."

Carter: "Ha, but there have been if you delve into the history of this two square mile area. Over the past few hundred years of history you'll find ships disappearing with no apparent reason and legends being told by the people of the islands that surround this area about vessels being found with no one aboard."

Harry: "I've heard these stories before. They're stories being told by people that heard the tales about other ships being found in the same way. It's became an urban legend in some parts of the world, someone finds a ship the crews gone never to be seen again. The story's typical."

Carter: "You're right Harry, but with one exception, these ships were covered in blood and in some cases body parts."

Harry: "Here's a simple explanation, pirates boarded the vessels and killed the crew. They sunk most of the ships and the ones they didn't sink they set adrift. Simple scare tactics."

Carter: "Maybe, but there's one problem with that explanation, the ships were never ransacked and all the valuables were still there."

Harry: "Alright professor, so what do you want from me?"

Carter: "I'm leading an expedition to investigate the area. I do know that this phenomenon only activates once every ninety years because of the research I have done. I know we can finally get some evidence of other worlds or dimensions, maybe even proof of the afterlife and I want you with me to witness the greatest discovery man has ever made."

Harry: "I'm sorry Professor, the answer's no. I've travelled the world for years and found nothing. This convinces me that there is nothing. It's time I stopped chasing ghosts and get on with my life."

Carter: "Please reconsider Harry, I need this one," he said with desperation in his voice.

Harry: "What are you talking about? You don't need this, you're a highly respected man in your field, why do you want to do this?"

Carter: "I'm dying. I've got about six months to a year left. This is my last chance to find out when I leave this world is there anything else out there for me."

Harry looked at Professor Carter. He could see that the Professor was upset and uncommonly desperate but Harry still refused to go on the expedition. As he turned to walk out of the office Professor Carter spoke:

"Please don't decide now, read my notes first and then decide. We'll be leaving in three days. If you're not at the airport by four-thirty Thursday morning then I'll have your final answer. No matter what happens, there will be no hard feelings on my part. I have decided that life's too short."

When Harry arrived home, he put Carter's notes on top of his coffee table. Harry had no intention of going over the professor's notes. Then he made himself something to eat and settled down to watch the television. Eventually he fell asleep.

At about two o'clock in the morning Harry awoke from a restless sleep and when he opened his eyes he glanced in the direction of the coffee table, or to be more precise Professor Carter's notes.

Maybe Harry felt sorry for the professor or maybe it was his curiosity getting the better of him, but he let out a sigh and went to the kitchen to brew a fresh pot of coffee. He returned to the living room and sat down, he stared at the professor's notes for a while, then reluctantly took them from the coffee table and started to read.

Over the next two days Harry went over the notes he read them three times. Harry couldn't fault the professor's research but according to the professor the phenomenon didn't start to activate for another ten to eleven years, so how does he expect to get any results, he thought to himself.

That evening, after putting a lot of thought into his decision, Harry decided to take Carter up on his offer. He went to his bedroom to get his passport and pack a suitcase, then he headed out the door and took a cab to the airport. 'If I hurry, I will still make it,' he thought to himself.

Harry soon got to the airport. He saw Carter and his team ready to board the plane. Harry shouted to Professor Carter and when Carter turned around Harry could see the look of joy on his face.

Carter beckoned him over and handed Harry a ticket. It felt like Carter knew Harry would be there, but then again the professor never could take no for an answer.

Harry slept for most of the flight, he awoke just before the plane was about to land and a while later they disembarked. Outside the airport there was transport waiting for them and they were driven to a small airfield located on the outer rim of the island.

There was what looked like a large cargo plane that had been converted into a sea plane sitting on the runway and to the left of that there were several large tents. Professor Carter lead everybody into one of the tents where they all sat down. Carter started to talk.

Carter: "I would first like to thank all of you for joining my little expedition, especially my friend Harry and again thank you all. I know that you are all excited to get started but we won't be able to get to the site for another two days, we have to wait till the weather has settled.

Harry: "I have a question professor."

Carter: "Go on Harry."

Harry: "In your notes you said that this anomaly only opened every ninety years or so for about six months each time."

Carter: "Yes the ships that disappeared and the ships that were found unmanned happened over the space of six months I've been back well over three hundred years' worth of history and each time the same thing happened. Every ninety years on the dot then around six months later it stopped. During the six months there were also reports of strange storms in that two mile area, but after that the stories get sketchy.

"It took me two years trying to sort out the truth from legend and even with that this is all still a long shot but we all knew this when we signed up for this expedition."

Harry: "Yes professor, but the question I would like you to answer is if it only starts every ninety years then we'll have to wait another ten or eleven years."

Carter: "Normally you would be right. So let me introduced you all to Doctor Bail. Doctor Bail has somewhat perfected a machine that maybe able to open the... shall we call it the door... for the lack of a better word. This could be the chance we are all looking for, the proof we have searched for all these years."

For two days Harry and the others got ready going over the plan over and over again, Harry could almost recite it in his sleep. The day came finally when they got the go ahead from Carter. It took about an hour to get to the coordinates and then Doctor Bail started up his machine.

It took a few minutes to start up properly and when it was at full power Bail pushed a large red button at the side of his device. What looked like a bolt of static power shot out of it. The static shot landed into the sea.

Harry: "Well, that was a bit of an anti-climax, wasn't it?"

Bail: "Wait for it, Harry, be patient."

Suddenly the sea below the plane became uneasy and restless, Above the plane, dark and unnatural storm clouds covered the godly light of the sun.

Carter and Bail started to cheer, the rest of them started to become uneasy as lightening started to flash from the heavy dark cloud cover. A strong wind started to rise and then began to rock the plane. Doctor Bail said that no one should worry, that this was to be expected and they were all perfectly safe.

As Harry looked out of the plane he saw in the distance what looked like a tyre on the horizon which slowly became a small hole and then it became a rip into what seemed to be another world.

All the Doctors on the plane, including Carter and Bail, were stunned at what they were witnessing. The man sitting beside Harry was Doctor Simons, he was giggling like a schoolgirl when suddenly he stopped and started to look around.

Harry: "Simons, what's wrong? You've gone very pale."

Simons: "Can you hear that?" he said with a fearful tone.

Bail: "Hear what? I can't hear anything."

Harry: "He's right there's no sound at all it's as quiet as a church at night and the plane isn't being tossed about."

Doctor Pascal who was sitting across from Harry jumped up from his set and shouted, "Jesus, look we're being dragged towards the opening."

Harry: "You're wrong. The opening has just got a bit bigger it's like we're in the eye of a storm it's alright that's why everything's so still and calm." As he said that Doctor's Lenard, Conrad and Reynolds agreed with Pascal.

Harry: "Ok professor, I think it's time we turned back. We got the pictures and the readings now you have all the proof you need you'll be remembered for a long time to come. Congratulations, now let's go."

Carter: "Yes maybe you're right," he said with a disappointed tone.

Then he turned to the pilot and started to talk to him in his own language. As Harry watched Carter and the pilot talking, the pilot seemed to be getting very angry with Professor Carter. They started to argue loudly, suddenly Carter grabbed the plane's steering control.

The plane started to fly out of control and Carter screamed out.

Carter: "He's gone mad he's trying to fly us into the rip. For god's sake someone help me. Oh no, it's too late."

He was right, the distortion was pulling the plane in and with the momentum of the uncontrolled plane there was no way it could be pulled out of the dive. They all started to scream as the plane went down. Harry watched out the window opposite where he was sitting and he was convinced he was going to die. Suddenly he closed his eyes and everything went black.

He could just about hear someone call his name as he opened his eyes. He realised that he had been unconscious. As he looked around he was in a daze and his sight was slightly blurred but what he could make out was the plane had crashed. He saw Pascal, Carter and Simons putting out small fires.

A few seconds later when Harry had composed himself he looked around. He looked up at where the doorway had closed behind them then he looked at the environment around him. The sky was a deep purple colour, the plants and fauna looked strange, everything was alive but at the same time seemed dead and there didn't seem to be any animal life. Harry thought to himself that this place was as close to hell as a mortal could come.

Harry: "Where the hell are we?"

Conrad: "Maybe we're dead, maybe we didn't survive the crash."

Carter: "No, we're still alive."

Lenard: "And how do you know that?" he said sarcastically.

Carter: "For one thing I've got a heartbeat and for another the pilot's the one who's dead. Anyway I think we're in the rip."

Harry walked around what was left of the plane. He saw the pilot with a large part of the windscreen imbedded in his skull.

Harry: "We have to bury the pilot then we can see what we can salvage from the wreckage."

Reynolds: "Look at this place it's wonderful but frightening."

They buried the pilot and broke up into pairs before starting to scout around the area. An hour went past when they all met back at the plane but Carter and Bail were missing.

Harry: "Where did they get to? We agreed to meet back here in an hour. Stay here I'll go and try to find them."

Pascal: "No we can't, we have to stay together. If they're not here soon we'll all search for them, we don't know much about this place."

Harry: "You're right, safety in numbers I suppose."

Three hours passed and there was still no sign of Doctor Bail and Professor Carter. At this point Harry and the others were getting ready to move out and search for them.

Lenard: "Can you hear that?"

Conrad: "SHHH he's right I can hear something."

They all stood there, still and quiet, when they heard Carter and Bail roaring that they had found something.

Harry and the others looked up and saw them excitedly running towards the wreckage.

Carter: "We've found something," he said with a hint of childish excitement in his voice. "Come on, lets go you must see it."

As Carter ran towards where he had come from they all followed him. About a half hour later Carter and Bail had led them to a graveyard of ships, not only old ships but aircraft from as early as the First World War and as late as the Second World War. In the distance they saw a battleship which couldn't have been more than fifteen-years-old. Harry recognised the name, the SS. Juliana, it was reported lost with all hands aboard thirteen years ago

Harry started to get worried, it looked like they weren't the only expedition that had the same idea of forcing the door open to this place. Harry had an idea that Professor Carter and Doctor Bail already knew this.

Harry: "Professor you knew you were going to find this didn't you? And what's more, you and Doctor Bail knew that what we had done had been done before. By the looks of some of those planes and ships it has already been attempted at least twice before."

Carter: "Yes, you're right Harry, nineteen forty-two and again thirteen years ago but there was no real proof that opening the door really worked now we do have proof."

Simons: "If you know so much about where we are then where the hell are we?"

Bail: "Here is what people normally refer to as the afterlife. This is where we come when we die. There is no heaven or hell just a world for the dead."

Reynolds: "You're crazy, if that were so where's everybody who died? What, no answer professor? The truth is you don't know where or what this place is. The pilot didn't try to land here, you did this, you stranded us here."

Harry: "We can put the blame where it belongs later but for now we need to find a way out of here. The first thing to do is to search the planes and ships, maybe we can find something to help us get the hell out of here."

They split up into groups and started to search. It took them almost a day and a half to search all of the vessels. When they had finished they met up at the edge of the graveyard.

Harry: "We found fire axes, ammo and guns but none of the guns work. There's nothing wrong with them but for some reason they still don't work."

Pascal: "Nothing works here."

Reynolds: "Maybe, but did you notice that the ships that are here have not decayed, not even the very old ones. They look like the day they were taken from the sea and what's even stranger is there are no bodies and what are all the missing ships and aircraft doing in this one spot? Who or what put them here?"

Lenard: "Yes they're all in one area except for ours, why?"

Pascal: "I may have a reason for that. I could swear earlier we were being pulled towards the rip but we weren't, we crashed. It could be that there are some strange forces that guide the aircraft and ships to this one spot."

Lenard: "If that's true we still have to worry about a force strong enough to transport a thousand ton battleship over two miles of land and not to mention what took the crews from these ships and planes."

Harry: "It's time we got back to the plane."

Carter: "We should stay here. There's plenty of cover and plenty of shelter. Back there we have nothing."

Harry: "Back at our plane we know the area and Doctor Bail may be able to fix his machine. Then we can open the door again and get the hell out of here. At least now we've got weapons. If there is something around we can protect ourselves."

Harry led the others back to the crash site and as they walked back he got the feeling that they were being watched. This place sent a cold shiver up his spine.

As they got to the crash site it was getting dark and Harry looked up into the sky. It was like someone had thrown a black blanket over the sky. There were no stars and no moon. Harry didn't like it one bit. In this place he got the feeling that it wasn't safe and when night fell he told the others to pick up any old wood lying around as they walked so that they could build a fire when they got back.

Later that night as Pascal and Bail lit the fire and everybody settled down to sleep, they heard a loud scream coming from the direction of where they had buried the pilot. Carter got up and took a lit piece of wood from the fire and started to walk when Harry grabbed him and pulled him back.

Harry: "Stay here, its too dark, there's a chance you might not find your way back. We'll wait till first light."

Suddenly they heard a loud deep growl coming from the dark and everybody jumped up and reached for an axe. The growl got louder and sounded nearer then it stopped just as suddenly as it started. They stood quietly and waited for a couple of minutes but there was still no sounds.

Simons: "There's nothing there, the fire probably scared it off," he said with a low whisper.

Then Simons took the lighted torch from Professor Carter and slowly walked to the edge of the glow from the fire. He waved the lit torch about a few times then he looked around at everybody and laughed.

Simons: "There's nothing there, you babies."

Before he could say anything else a large beast came leaping from the darkness and dragged Simons to the ground. Whatever it was, it was big, hairy and had a mouth full of large razor-sharp teeth.

It took Simon's head off with one bite and proceeded to maul the rest of his body using its teeth to shred the flesh from it. There were bits of him hanging from between the animal's teeth and a pool of blood formed around the lifeless corpse.

They took the axes and started to hit the beast but the axes didn't even make a dent. The beast stood there feeding on Simon's corpse as if they weren't even there. It didn't see them as much of a threat.

Then the beast turned around and looked at them. Harry could swear that the beast grinned at him.

It poised as it was getting ready to attack. A humanoid figure ran towards the beast from the darkness he jumped onto its back and the beast ran into the darkness with the figure on his back. A few seconds later they heard a blood-curdling scream.

Everything went deathly quiet then slowly the figure walked into the light. It was a man covered in blood and the clothes he was wearing looked like what was once a military uniform. He had a large knife in his hand dripping with the blood of the beast, then he spoke.

Man: "You're safe now it's dead, they won't bother you anymore tonight they don't like the smell of their own dead."

Reynolds: "Who are you?"

Man: "Petty Officer Bud Leland of the SS. Juliana."

He walked over to the fire and sat down, Bud looked intensely into the flames as if he had gone into a trance.

Harry: "Would you like something to eat Bud?"

Bud turned and looked at Harry. He started to laugh, then he broke down in tears. They all looked at him as he rubbed his eyes.

Bud: "I'm sorry folks I haven't seen or spoken to another living soul in just over ten years I think and yes I wouldn't mind something to eat, thank you."

After Bud had eaten, Harry and the others introduced themselves. Harry asked how come he was here and what happened to the other members of his crew.

Bud: "Thirteen years ago the government was testing what we thought was a new weapon. We didn't know what this weapon did. We were there just as spectators and we had some high profile politicians on board.

"When the scientists triggered the weapon, they somehow opened a gate into a paranormal world. We thought we were far enough away but we were wrong, the ship was pulled in through the gate and as it happened the whole crew passed out.

"When we woke up there was no water under us, just land, and all around us there were ships and planes everywhere. Then we saw planes, everything from World War Two all the way back about three to four hundred years. It was amazing. We weren't worried we expected to be rescued within three days to a week but the one thing we didn't know was that there wasn't going to be a rescue. They abandoned us."

Carter: "What about your crew? Where are they and how many of them are there?"

Bud: "My crew consisted of one hundred and fifty-three men including the captain, four scientists and three highly important politicians."

Bail: "What do you mean consisted of? That doesn't sound good."

Bud: "They're all dead or missing."

Harry: "What happened to them?"

Bud: "We were here about two weeks without incident, the scientists took readings, plant samples, soil samples and water samples all the scientific crap. We investigated all the abandoned ships and planes they were empty.

"There was no one about so we started to explore our surroundings. That's when the men started to disappear. It took two nights to figure out that we were being hunted by the indigenous wildlife but we were lucky they only came out at night.

"They were hard to kill, not even our bullets could pierce their skin, then something unforeseen happened, our guns stopped working for no apparent reason. We found out later that whatever was here maybe something in the air rendered the gunpowder useless over time.

"The captain ordered us to make weapons out of anything that wasn't screwed down so we did. After that it was getting harder to fight the creatures off the only thing in our favour was they couldn't climb the side of the ship. They didn't even try, it was like they were waiting, but about our third week in somehow one of them got on board and attacked the captain. Before he died he stuck the animal with a large galley knife.

"The ship's doctor performed an autopsy on the animal. Under their skin was like a suit of armour, the bone was thick all over it and nearly as hard as steel except in two places, in the joints at the top of the front legs, you get a knife in there and it's over. All we had to do is avoid their teeth and we were fine. Then when we were through with the creature's corpse we dumped it overboard they didn't come around after that. That's how we found out that they seemed frightened of their own dead."

Conrad: "So they killed all your crew?"

Bud: "No, only about sixteen of them."

Carter: "Then what the hell killed the rest of them then?"

Bud: "Monsters that used to be men not dead and not alive. They feed on the living."

Lenard: "Are you trying to tell us that zombies inhabit this place and we're going to be eaten? You expect me to believe this shit?"

Bud: "No don't be stupid flesh-eating zombies are make-believe, Hollywood fantasy, but if it were that we would be relatively safe. These things are something different they are somewhat intelligent they're not mindless husks."

Harry: "What are they then?"

Bud: "I don't know but I do know that they were once people like us. I caught one in a trap about eight years ago and I interrogated it. All it would say is it's soul was given to the dark one and that eventually it and it's kind would feast on mine and when the time came they would escape from their prison and it and it's kind will gorge themselves on the souls of the world. That's when I knew we torn a hole open from our world into hell but I think you all know that already."

Harry: "We'll get out of here Bud, and we'll take you with us."

Bud: "Good luck with that pal, to coin a phrase, you haven't got a snowball's chance in hell."

Harry: "We have the devise that we used to get here. Maybe we can get it running again."

Bud: "Maybe, how long have you been here?"

Pascal: "Not even twenty-four hours."

Bud: "Then we have a chance. We have just less than two weeks."

Bail: "What happens in two weeks?"

Bud: "After that time any power source you have becomes useless, it's like this place drains all the energy from any manmade object. We'll start tomorrow, tonight we rest."

Carter: "Earlier there was a scream was it you?"

Bud: "That wasn't me, did anybody die today?"

Conrad: "Yes, our pilot died during the crash."

Bud: "Shit, they know you're here in this godforsaken place. The soul stays in the body it can't escape. The soul-suckers must have smelt him they won't stop till we're all dead and they have taken our essence."

Harry: "What do you mean soul-suckers?"

Bud: "That's what I call them because that's what they do, they feast on your soul."

Carter: "So who screamed?"

Bud: "Your pilot. To him they were eating him alive. He'll suffer like that for an eternity."

Carter started to pace up and down and mutter to himself. Harry could hear him saying that this was total bullshit and that he was screwed.

Bud: "Don't worry friend, if this is hell like those things believe, then there's definitely a heaven."

Bud whispered to Harry.

Bud: "What's his problem?"

Harry: "He's dying, he's only got a short time left cancer I think."

Bud: "Why didn't you tell me that?"

Harry: "Why what does it matter?"

Bud: "He's going to become one of them, it's happened before. One of the scientists aboard ship was dying, it was like a virus. It started attacking his body from when we got here because he was already dying. To this world he was the same as the soul-suckers, neither dead nor alive. So he changed, he kept it quiet and before we knew what was happening he sucked eighteen of my crew mates dry."

Carter: "Oh god no, why did I come here?" he said with a panicked tone.

Harry: "We'll keep an eye on him. If he changes I'll personally put him down."

Bud: "You people still don't get it, they can't be killed at least while they're awake."

Harry: "So they can be killed."

Bud: "Yes, sleep is their only weakness."

Bail: "Then why have you not killed them all off?"

Bud: "Do you think we hadn't tried? I lost fifty good men over the years trying to find out where their lair was located and I've been looking for years by myself the only thing in our favour is that they're no stronger than us physically unless they're in a pack. But we can subdue the professor when the time comes and if we get him out of here quickly enough before the transformation is complete he may return to normal."

Carter: "What if we don't get out in time? What happens to me then?"

Bud: "We leave you here. If just one of those things gets out into our world there's no telling what damage it could do."

Harry: "What do these things look like?"

Bud: "Just like us except when they feed they change into something horrible and watching them feed is no pleasant sight."

Conrad: "Then we'd better get started as soon as possible."

Bud: "We'll head back to the Juliana at first light now get some sleep."

The next morning when they awoke they saw a thick mist covering everything. Doctor Bail and Professor Carter were taking an inventory of parts that were needed for Bail's machine and when they had finished Bud led them back to the SS. Juliana.

As they walked through the ship's graveyard the mist started to dissipate as they were approaching the Juliana. Just then two men suddenly appeared in their path, their faces pale white, their eyes black and devoid of humanity.

One of them stretched out his arm and pointed at Reynolds. Then he smiled.

Bud: "Not too bad, there are only two of them. When I tell you to, run as fast as you can towards the rope ladders on the Juliana, I can hold them off."

One of the soul-suckers opened his mouth and let out an ungodly screech and about ten of them jumped from the surrounding ships.

Bud: "Shit, ran!" he cried

They all ran for the Juliana as fast as they could and scrambled up the ladder. As Doctor Reynolds got to the rope ladder one of the soul-suckers grabbed him and threw him to the ground. The others gathered around him and their faces became distorted. A thick black oil-like substance came spurting from their open mouths and covered Reynolds. Then a loud deep voice came from the mist, a large man stepped into view. He seemed to be different from the others, more in control.

The soul-suckers then did something strange. Their faces returned to normal and they stepped away from Reynolds.

He walked to where Reynolds was lying, he bent down and picked him up off the ground then he slowly looked up at Harry and the others. Harry turned to Bud.

Harry: "This boy gives me the creeps, who is he?"

Bud: "He's their leader he calls himself Legend. This one can change anyone he feeds on into one of him."

Conrad: "Why do they not come up here and get us? There are enough of them."

Bud: I don't know they never rushed the ship I suppose they didn't have to."

Harry: "What do you want from us?" he asked Legend.

Legend: "I want the key."

Pascal: "What key what are you talking about?"

Legend: "Open the door so we can pass through. Turn the key and let us out or you will die slowly. If you do as I have asked you will be given your lives as a reward. Give me your answer now."

Bud: "Go to hell."

Legend: "Very disappointing, Until you give me what I want this will be your fate."

Legend looked at Doctor Reynolds then he threw him to the ground the other soul-suckers surrounded him and as before, the soul-suckers faces distorted. Reynolds repeatedly begged them not to kill him but they seemed to get more excited the more frightened that Reynolds had got.

The soul-suckers seemed to be extracting Reynolds' life force. What Harry and the others saw next sickened them to the core. While Reynolds was still alive they started to feed on his flesh. They could hear him screaming with every lump of flesh torn from his body.

Legend: "Heed my warning, give me what I want or your fate will be worse than his. I will make sure of it."

Then he disappeared back into the fog as the other soul-suckers devoured what was left of Reynolds' mutilated corpse then skulked back into the mist.

Harry: "We could have done something to help him."

Bud: "No we could do nothing that black stuff they covered him in would have killed him. Anyway he would have died of a slow and more painful death if we had got him away from them."

Lenard: "what was that stuff?"

Bud: "I think it breaks the body down so they can feed."

Pascal: "here wait a minute, you told us that they feed on the soul of a person not the body."

Bud: "The nearest I can figure out is that they have tainted souls like a hole inside them and the only way they can fill that hole is by draining the essence from another but they must feed their bodies too and they've got a taste for human flesh."

Bail: "So when there's no human flesh around what do they eat?"

Bud: "The animals that attacked you last night, that's what they were bred for, but the soul-suckers prefer humans."

Carter: "How have you survived for so long?"

Bud: "I use the dead blood of the beasts to smear my body, it helps keep them of my scent. The soul-suckers despise the smell of death just like the beasts, that's why they eat their pray alive and that's the reason why there are no bodies."

Harry: "But our pilot was dead."

Bud: "The pilot's essence was too tempting. You don't really die here. Well your body dies but what you are doesn't. Anyway enough talk where do we start with this machine of yours?"

Bail: "I need these parts," he handed a list to Bud.

Bud: "Go to the machine shop if you can't find the items there we'll have to improvise we'll take pieces from the ship."

For two days they all pitched in to help repair Doctor Bail's device. Just as it was getting dark on the second night Carter called everybody together.

Carter: "We think it's finished all we have to do is test the machine. Over to you Doctor Bail."

Bail started to push buttons on the device just as he did on the plane, but nothing happened. He tried again and still nothing happened. He opened a small hatch at the side of the machine and started to look inside.

A few minutes later Bail sat down with a bewildered look on his face. Harry asked him what happened.

Bail: "The power converter's gone."

Pascal: "Maybe it dropped out when we were moving it from the plane to here."

Bail: "It couldn't have, when that part's inserted into the machine it self-secures."

Lenard: "It could have jarred loose during the crash."

Bail: "I suppose there is a small chance it could have come loose and fell out, but we need that converter the device won't work without it," he said worriedly.

Bud: "Just make another one, I'm sure we can scrounge the materials somewhere."

Bail: "No, you don't understand, I can't build one. It was specially made this is the only one in existence. If we can't find it we're stuck here."

Carter: "Then we have to find it, we have to get out of here," he said excitedly and in a panic.

Harry: "Calm down professor, we'll find it, we'll search the ship first and if it isn't here we'll trace our steps. Let's hope we find it here I don't fancy going out there unless I have to. Doctor Bail, what does the converter look like?"

Bail: "What were looking for is a round silver sphere about the size of a clenched fist with several flashing red green and blue lights around it. The converter is in that sphere."

Suddenly Professor Carter put his hands over his face and dropped to his knees. He let out a blood-curdling roar as he took his hands down from his face and looked at them. It looked as of the life was being drained from his features. Then Carter jumped to his feet and grabbed Doctor Pascal by the throat and started to choke him. Bud lifted a piece of copper piping from a table and hit professor Carter on the back of the head. The professor fell to the floor. He rolled onto his back and his face changed to its normal state.

Bud: "It's started. He's starting to change. I'm sorry but we have to lock him up for his own safety and own."

Harry: "Look we need his help, we can't do this on our own."

Carter: "Harry don't, he's right, I'm getting dangerous, but I can still help it'll just be behind a closed door."

They locked Carter in one of the staterooms and they searched the ship for three hours. They all met in the mess hall but none of them had any luck finding the converter."

Harry: "We need to go outside and trace our steps."

Bud: "We can't all go some of us have to stay here. Harry, Lenard, Conrad, Pascal and I will go and look for the power converter. Doctor Bail you stay here and look after Professor Carter. If we're not back here within four to five hours there's a chance we'll not be back."

Bud, Harry, Lenard, Conrad and Pascal started out at first light. They walked slowly from the ship to the crash site but there was no sign of the power converter.

Conrad: "Maybe it's in the plane."

They searched in and around the plane from top to bottom three times but there was no converter.

Conrad: "They have the converter, they must have found it. We're doomed, we're never going to get out of here. We're going to be slaughtered by those devils."

Harry: "Don't be so dramatic Conrad, if they have it we'll get it back somehow."

Bud: "The soul-suckers don't have it."

Pascal: "How do you know for certain they don't have it?"

Bud: "It was one of us, I've seen it before some people give up and they give themselves over to legend. The soul-suckers would have tried to make some sort of deal but we haven't seen hide nor hair of Legend or the other soul-suckers in two days."

Lenard: "Well that is until now." Then he pointed to the sand dune behind them. One of the soul-suckers was perched on top of a rock like a bird of prey.

He looked down at them then cocked it's head back and started to screech like some sort of wild animal. Just then four more of them appeared.

The one that was perched on the rock pointed at them and then turned to the other soul-suckers and let out a loud scream and they went running towards them.

Bud: "Run like the devil was after you, in all directions. We'll meet back at ship."

As Harry was running he could hear screams in the distance. He eventually got back to the ship with his heart pounding like thunder in his chest. He found it hard to breathe. Doctor Bail run towards him.

Bail: "Are you all right Harry?"

Harry: "Yes, I'm fine."

Bail: "Where's the others?" he said as he looked around.

Harry: "What they aren't back yet?" he asked surprisingly.

Then he remembered as he was running for his life that he had heard some of the others screaming.

Bail: "I'll keep an eye out just in case," he said quietly with a hint of both fear and disappointment in his voice.

Bail: "Did you find the power converter," he said nervously.

Harry: "No there was no sign of it anywhere. Bud thought that one of us removed the converter, maybe he was right one of us may have wanted to make a bargain."

Bail: "It makes no difference now, if we can't get the converter back we're stuck here."

The two men sat on the deck of the Juliana quietly as it was getting dark. They could hear someone shouting, "Let the ladder down, for god's sake hurry up."

Harry and Bail ran to the other side of the ship. They looked out into the darkness and saw Pascal and Bud running towards the ship. They got to the ladders and climbed onto the deck and collapsed panting for breath.

Harry lent over Pascal.

Harry: "The others, Conrad, Lenard did you see them?"

Pascal: "No I haven't seen anyone since we started running. I never looked back. The only one I've seen was Bud and that was only a few minutes ago, but I did hear someone scream a few minutes after we parted," he said, while trying to catch his breath.

Harry: "What about you Bud, did you see any of the others?"

Bud: "No, but I did hear the screams that Pascal heard."

Harry: "We'll watch out for them."

Bud: "You do realise that there's a ninety-nine percent chance that they're dead?"

Harry: "I know but we have to have some faith."

Bud: "Ok I'll keep watch."

Harry went to the state room where they had placed Professor Carter. He unlocked and opened the door. The lights were out and the room was in total darkness. He called to Carter but there was no answer. With a tremor in his tone he called out again.

Suddenly Carter came charging out of the darkness at him. Harry fell to the ground as Carter grabbed him by the hair and held him down. Carter's face became distorted as he opened his mouth. At that moment Harry knew that he was going to die but as Carter was about to extract Harry's essence he suddenly stopped and his face returned to normal.

Carter: "Oh my god, I'm sorry Harry, it's getting harder to fight. I can feel something growing inside me and I can't control it I'm so hungry."

Harry: "It's ok professor, don't worry about it, no harm done."

Carter: "Did you find the converter?"

Harry: "No, Bud thinks that one of us took it to save their own lives – a bargaining tool, I suppose."

Carter: "It makes sense, self-preservation is a strong and powerful motive. Now close the door and lock it don't open it again until we are ready to go."

Harry: "There's something else, Conrad and Lenard are missing."

Carter: "What happened?"

Harry: "We went to look for the power converter and ended up at the crash site. We were attacked and got separated."

Carter: "Hopefully they're fine and they'll make their way back in one piece."

Harry: "Ok professor, I had better get back to the others."

Carter: "Harry can you give me some reading material? I need to keep my mind focused and I brought all my notes with me. I need to go over them again I may find something I missed."

Harry: "I'll be back in a while with your notes."

Harry then closed and locked the door. As he walked up to the deck he heard Bail calling for him and he ran to where Bail and the others were standing.

Harry: "What's wrong?"

Bud: "It's Legend, he has Conrad."

Legend: "Give me the key, give it to me now!" he roared with anger.

Conrad: "Go to hell you son of a bitch."

Harry: "Where's Lenard? What have you done with him?"

Legend: "Come here," he shouted, as he looked into the darkness.

As he had called out Lenard walked into sight. He stood there and stared up at Harry and the others.

Legend: "Give me the key to your world."

Bail: "No we can't do that. I'm sorry Conrad, Lenard, we can't risk these things getting to our world."

Legend: "Kill him – no, wait, you two go back to your friends let it be known that I have compassion," he said as he disappeared into the darkness.

As Harry and the others watched, to their surprise, the soul-suckers disappeared into the night. They didn't try to stop Lenard and Conrad from boarding the ship. Harry rushed over to help them on board. Conrad fell to his knees on the deck, he was clearly upset but Lenard on the other hand was unusually calm."

Harry: "Are you alright Lenard?"

There was no answer so Harry walked towards Lenard. Suddenly Lenard grabbed him, his face was distorted. Legend had turned him. Bud reacted straight away he ran over and grabbed Lenard then threw him overboard.

Lenard: "Give him what he wants, or you will end up like the others."

Then he started to laugh and he walked over to one of the planes and reached under one of the wings. He picked something up and held it above his head. It was the power converter.

Harry: "It was Lenard, he took the converter and made a deal. If you could call that a deal stupid asshole."

Conrad: "What are we going to do now?"

Harry: "I don't know."

Conrad: "This is bullshit we're all going to die."

While Conrad was panicking and pacing up and down they could hear a strange whistling sound and they all stopped. Conrad was still ranting when suddenly the whistling stopped with a thud and Doctor Conrad went silent. He looked down to see that was some sort of harpoon that had been thrust through his chest. He looked at the others with a look of surprise and bewilderment on his face.

Before Harry and the others could respond he was pulled backwards over the side of the ship then they heard Legend roar from the darkness, "You're running out of time."

The next morning they were talking about what they were going to do.

Harry: "I think Professor Carter should be included in this conversation."

Bail: "No, he's becoming one of them we can't trust him."

Bud: "Bail's right we can't trust him he's too dangerous. He could turn on us at any time."

Harry: "Nonetheless he's in this just as deep as we are, besides we need him."

Bud: "Ok but one wrong move and I will take his head off."

Harry: "Fine, do we have any cuffs we need to secure him."

Bud: "I'll get them. I'll meet you at the wardrooms."

When Bud reached the wardroom where Carter was being held the others were waiting outside.

Bud: "Here are the restraints," he said, as he threw the cuffs to the floor.

Harry picked up the cuffs then he unlocked the door. As he opened it he noticed that the light was off and he remembered what happened last time. He called out to Professor Carter nervously.

Carter: "It's all right Harry, I'm fine for the moment. So what do I owe the pleasure of this group visit? I thought that all of you had forgotten about me – well except for my good friend Harry of course," he said sarcastically.

Bud: "Harry thinks you can be helpful. I don't, so prove me wrong or I'll lock the door and you can rot in here."

Carter: "In what way do you think I can help?"

Harry: "Legend has the converter we have the machine, if we give him the machine we're either dead or stranded here, but if we don't give it to him we're just dead so what do you think we should do?"

Carter: "Are we all that's left?"

Harry: "Yes."

Carter: "I take it Lenard and Conrad didn't come back."

Harry: "They came back alright, Legend turned Lenard into one of the soul-suckers."

Carter: "Oh god. What about Conrad?"

Pascal: "When we wouldn't give Legend the machine, he let them go. What we didn't know was that Lenard had been changed. Bud fired him overboard. Conrad's dead too, they impaled him with a harpoon and dragged him off the ship. It's only us left."

Bud: "OK they're gone, but we're still here, so can you help or not?" he said angrily.

Carter: "Give them the machine."

Bail: "Have you lost your mind?"

Carter: "No, I haven't. They want to open the doorway to our world but even with the machine working they can't use it. Only Doctor Bail and I know how to operate it. We'll give them the machine and we'll take them with us but only under our terms."

Pascal: "They hold all the cards so why would they agree to our terms? They have us by the balls."

Harry: "The Professor's right, Lenard must have told him by now that there isn't much time left."

Carter: "Precisely if Doctor Bail and I agree to help them, if we all have safe passage out of here they'll have no choice but to, or deal."

Bud: "That's what we don't want. What's to stop them from killing or turning us as soon as we leave through the rift."

Carter: "I suspect that the ordinary soul-suckers don't have the same life expectancy in our world as they do here. I think they can be killed in our world."

Bud: "And what makes you so sure? Maybe they get stronger."

Carter: "I'm not sure of anything but I don't think so, it's just a guess but Legend doesn't seem the type to create anything stronger than him. It seems to me it's this place that keeps them from dying. It rejuvenates them somehow in my opinion the only one to watch out for is Legend. He seems to be the only one that can create these things so he may be an exception to the rule."

Harry: "So what now?"

Carter: "We wait. When they come back we make a deal. We're going to need help to make some sort of raft to carry the device and us to the opening, so why not let them do all the work and while they're doing that we can figure out a way to stop Legend from getting through the rift when we're on the other side. We can get rid of the rest ourselves."

Pascal: "But if you're wrong."

Harry: "Then we're screwed but it's the only plan we have."

Bud: "I suppose it's better than nothing, but I still don't trust you professor, you could turn at any time and give the game away."

Carter: "But I have an idea I could feel myself turning last night then I tried to kill myself by smashing my skull against the wall, but all I managed to do was knock myself senseless. Being dazed seemed to stop the change temporarily. My mind needs to be slowed way down it seems to make whatever is growing inside me vulnerable."

Bud: "So what?"

Carter: "Harry could give me something to slow me down. There's an eighty percent chance that it would slow the change to a crawl. Now I can start to feel it coming on. Each time I do Harry can dope me up. It may buy me some time."

Harry took a mid-strength sedative from the ship's hospital and injected it into Carter's arm. The sedative started to work immediately and they took off the cuffs slowly.

Carter: "Good, I can't feel anything. I was right, as time goes on you may have to up the dosage."

Bail: "It'll kill you if we keep pumping that stuff into you."

Carter: "Not if, not if..." he said with a slurred voice as he started to doze off.

Pascal: "Professor wake up."

Carter: "WHAT? Oh yes, where was I? Yes it won't kill me, at least, not here. This place won't let me die just keep injecting me."

Harry and the others waited for hours. At last they could hear Legend shouting. Harry went to the bottom deck and looked over the railing.

Legend: "Have you come to a decision yet?"

Harry: "Yes we'll give you the device but the only ones who know how to operate it won't help you unless you give your word that we will not be left here and that we will not be harmed in any way, shape or form."

Legend: "You think you can tell me what to do. I tell you!" he said angrily.

Harry: "In another few days there will be no power to get the device to work so we're all running out of time, so what will it be."

The deformed Lenard walked over to Legend and started to whisper into his ear Legend looked up at Harry.

Legend: "You have your deal. Here's what you need the silver ball," he said as he dropped it onto the sandy ground.

As Legend started to walk into the darkness Harry shouted to him.

Legend: "What do you want?"

Harry: "We need help with transport to the beach for the device and again from the beach to the open water for the device and passengers.

Legend: "It will be ready in two days, have the key operational then."

Then he disappeared into the night. Harry climbed down the rope ladder and slowly and carefully walked over to the power converter. He lifted it and then headed back to the ship.

He carried it to Doctor Bail. The Doctor took about ten minutes to fit it into place then he nervously started the test. After the test was over he smiled.

Bail: "It's one hundred percent, we're ready I have set it for a short duration. This means the door will only open for a few minutes, hopefully it will be enough time for us to escape. But how do we stop Legend?"

Carter: "Leave that to me I have an idea."

Two days went by without incident. Towards the middle of the second day they heard Legend roar, "It's time!"

Harry and what was left of the scientific team carried the device down to a makeshift sand sled. They sat it carefully on the sled, and about a dozen soul-suckers took up chains and started to pull the sled through the sand.

A couple of hours later they arrived at the beach on the water's edge where there were two large rowing boats. They put the device in one and there was still room for Harry and the others. They started to get in when Legend grabbed Harry by the arm.

Legend: "You sit with me, you can explain what they are doing."

As Harry was led to the second boat, Professor Carter stood in their way.

Carter: "Where are you taking him?"

Legend: "He's coming with me just to make sure you stick to your part of the deal and he can tell me exactly what you and your friends are doing."

Carter: "That's fine with me, but Harry doesn't have a clue about what we're doing."

Legend: "Then who else can tell me how the device works?"

Carter: "I will be glad to, but I'll only explain it as Doctor Bail executes the system."

Legend: "That would be satisfactory."

Carter: "Harry, go and sit with the others."

Harry: "But professor."

Carter: "Don't but me, just do as you're told."

It was then that Harry knew that Professor Carter was going to sacrifice himself to save the rest of us.

As Carter turned to walk away Harry could see a smile forming on his lips.

Pascal: "Where's Carter going?"

Harry whispered so that the two soul-suckers that where rowing the boat wouldn't hear him.

Harry: "He's going to try to slow Legend down and buy us some time." Then he let out a deep sigh.

Bail started to operate the machine just as he did before. A few minutes later a hole began to form, it started to get wider and as soon as the rift was big enough to go through Harry looked back and saw Carter waving to him.

As the boats where being dragged towards the rift Harry pushed one of the soul-suckers off the boat then Pascal grabbed the other one. They started to struggle before Harry could help Pascal and the soul-sucker fell overboard. Harry tried to grab Pascal but the rowing boat was being pulled too fast towards the rip. Harry looked back at Professor Carter opening his coat. Carter had strapped explosives to his chest, then suddenly there was a large explosion.

Harry looked up, there was no sign of the Professor or Legend as Harry, Bail, and Bud passed through the rift from that hell world into their own. Harry thought about the people that had died and then started to weep.

Then Bail put his hand on Harry's shoulder.

Bail: "It's alright you did the best you could. Now it's time to rest."

Harry looked around at Doctor Bail and Bud and to his horror Bail's face became distorted and his eyes were black and void of humanity. Bud sat at the back of the boat looking intensely at Harry and smiling.

Bud: "Go ahead Doctor you earned the first bite." Then he started to cackle wildly.

Bail let out a loud high-pitched scream then started to laugh.

Harry: "O JESUS GOD NOOOOO."

THE END

SURVIVING THE DEAD

Connor O'Brian is an ordinary family man. He lives in a good area in a five-bedroom house with his wife Elaine and his three children Louise, Dominic and Sara.

He does the same thing every day. Gets up early in the morning and goes to work, comes home and goes to bed; every day's the same. This is his story of survival.

One day you're getting on with your life doing things that you normally take for granted like doing the shopping, paying the bills, going to work and taking care of your family, and the next you're running for your life.

It all started November the fifteenth 2014. The alarm went off at 7:00 in the morning as usual and I got out of bed got washed and dressed then went downstairs to the kitchen.

I sat at the breakfast table as Elaine put my usual on the table; three rounds of toast, a boiled egg and a strong cup of coffee. Then Sara and Dominic came into the kitchen, full of beans as usual, laughing and messing about.

Connor: "Where's Louise? Is she up yet?"

Elaine: "I woke her, she never does as she's told these days."

Connor: "You forget what we were like when we were that age, it was no picnic for our parents either."

Elaine: "It's not the same thing, she's getting out of hand."

Connor: "Elaine give her a break, be patent with her, she'll come round."

Elaine: "You don't know what you're talking about. You're away all day I have to put up with all the tantrums and all the abuse. I wish you would back me up sometimes and not take Louise's part," she said angrily.

Connor: "Ok I'll speak to her when I get home we'll get this sorted out I promise sweetheart. Now I'd better go to work or I'll be late and if that happens Jerry has another chance to make a fool out of me in front of everybody."

Elaine: "Maybe you should quit I don't like that Jerry; he's always looking at me with those beady eyes."

Connor: "I can't quit, you know that, as for Jerry looking at you, I couldn't blame him he fancy's you, there was a reason why I married the best looking girl around."

Elaine: "Oh go to work," she said as she laughed.

I kissed Elaine and walked to the front door before I left I shouted to Louise to get up or she'd be late. "Ok I'm coming now," she roared.

I got into the car and headed off to work. As I was driving, the news was on, the reporter said that there were sudden outbreaks of violence in parts of the city. It was nothing surprising in this day and age but I was paying more attention to the size of the traffic jam ahead.

I eventually got to work a few minutes late because of the traffic but try telling that to Jerry Cullen, my boss, a small fat balding man with delusions of grandeur. He acted as if he owned the place.

He's the kind of man that takes credit for everybody's good ideas. He probably never had an original idea of his own.

Jerry had it in for me only a few weeks after we met. All because I was moving up the ladder a lot faster than he was. He had a habit of intimidating people who might have had a future in the company. They either quit or he found an excuse to fire them.

But what really pissed him off about me was that I couldn't be intimidated and he couldn't find a good enough reason to hand me my cards. Probably because some of the higher ups had noticed me, to be truthful. Sometimes it made my day to know that he thought that I was a threat to his authority.

As I walked in, lo and behold, who did I run into? None other than Jerry.

Jerry: "O'Brian, what time do you call this, you're ten minutes late."

Connor: "I was caught in traffic, it wasn't my fault."

Jerry: "Of course it's your fault, all you have to do is leave your house a little earlier in the future and get in on time or I'll have to let you go, do you understand O'Brian?" he said with a hint of pleasure in his voice.

Everybody was watching as I walked to my office. It was so embarrassing. All I wanted to do was crawl under a rock and stay there for the rest of my life.

As I worked on my computer I was still fuming over that little show Jerry put on and all because he wanted to show everybody that he was the boss and I was nothing but his employee. What a tit.

I soon put it out of my mind and got on with my work. At about one o'clock I headed to the canteen. I sat down and opened my lunch box and in it were sandwiches that Elaine had made for me.

As I started to eat I looked at the television and the news was on. There was a report about a widespread string of violence and attacks.

There was nothing strange about violence in this day and age. What was strange was the elevation of these attacks all over the country and all in a twenty-four hour period. After lunch I thought no more about it and I put it down to my imagination.

At the end of the day I left work and I decided to take the back roads home to avoid the heavy traffic. As I was driving I fancied a bit of music and I just took my eyes off the road for a few seconds when I felt a thud.

I put my foot hard on the brake pedal and the car came to a screeching halt. My first instinct was to drive on but I knew that I would never be able to live with myself if I did that.

I got out of the car to see what – or god forbid who –I had hit. It was getting dark so I went to the trunk and took out a torch but when I shone it up the road there was nothing.

I walked to the front of the car. There was nothing there but I did hit something, the windshield was cracked, the bonnet was dented and there was blood on the broken headlight. Oh my god what have I done, I thought to myself.

I looked down the road again but there was nothing. I decided to search the ditches and as I did I prayed that it was an animal I had hit and not a person.

I walked down the road carefully looking for what I had hit. Suddenly I heard a groan coming from behind me on the other side of the road.

I slowly walked over when I got to the spot where I heard the groan, I stooped down and shone the torch into the ditch. I saw a body. There were chunks of flesh missing from his face and there was no way my car could have done that.

I was ashamed to think it but I was relieved to know that I couldn't have done this. I put my hand down to check this poor guy's pulse. There was none, he was dead.

Suddenly he jumped up and grabbed me. He tried to bite me but I pushed him to the ground and I looked him in the eyes which they were cold and dead. I backed off slowly but he jumped up and let out a horrifying scream then he ran for me. I turned and bolted to my car, got in and locked the doors. I tried to start the car but it didn't start and by this time the mutilated man was beating his fists on the window.

I tried to start the car again and it worked. Just as I started to drive the man broke through the window, I pushed him hard and he fell to the ground. As I was driving I looked out of my rear view mirror and in the distance I could see the man stand up. How could he have done that, he was dead I was sure of it.

When I got home I parked the car in my driveway. It was eerily quiet as

I stepped out of the car and looked around. The street was deserted and in the distance I could hear screaming.

I hurried to the front door and went in. I called out to Elaine, but there was no answer. I run into the living room Elaine was on the chair watching the news on television. Se looked like she was in shock as she looked around at me with horror in her eyes.

Connor: "Elaine, I called out did you not hear me?"

Elaine: "Have you seen the news? This must be some kind of joke."

Connor: "I saw it earlier. There's been attacks and widespread violence. Why, what are they saying now?"

Elaine: "They're saying that people are returning from the dead and they're attacking the living. The media's calling them zombies. It can't be true, there's no such thing, there can't be, these thing's only exist in movies don't they Connor?"

Connor "This morning I would have agreed with you, but now I'm not so sure. When I was driving home I hit something. I got out and took a look to see what I had hit and one of them attacked me. I just about got away. Where's the kids?"

Elaine: "Upstairs. I don't think they know anything about what's going on."

Connor: "Good we'll keep it that way for now I'll go check on them."

I headed up the stairs to the bedrooms. Dominic and Sara were in Dominic's room playing with the computer. Then I knocked Louise's bedroom door but there was no answer. She probably didn't hear me because of that racket the kids call music these days.

I knocked again and called out her name but there was still no answer. I walked in and looked around, she wasn't in her room and the window was open. I looked out of it there was no sign of her.

I closed the window and hurried quickly downstairs. When I entered the sitting room Elaine was sitting on the chair shaking with fear.

Connor: "Where's Louise? She isn't in her room."

Elaine: "She must have sneaked out. We had an argument earlier, she wanted to go to her friend's house and I wouldn't let her because she refused to her homework and then I sent her to her room."

Conner: "Can you remember which friend it was?"

Elaine: "She didn't say."

A few minutes later the phone started to ring. I lifted the receiver, it was Louise, she sounded frightened.

Connor: "What's wrong Louise?"

Louise: "Dad I'm scared."

Connor: "Ok calm down, tell me where you are and what's going on."

Louise: "I'm in June's house. Her dad's gone mental. He attacked us, he bit June's mum. He bit a lump of flesh right off her arm. Then we ran."

Connor: "Where are you now and who's with you?"

Louise: "I'm in the attic. There's me, June, her mum Mary and June's Uncle Tim."

Connor: "Ok make sure you bar the door properly and I'll be there soon. Just keep your head and don't panic."

Louise: "Ok dad I'm sorry." Then she started to cry.

Connor: "Don't worry we'll sort all that out when I get you back home safe and sound."

Then I heard a loud banging sound and Louise screaming.

Connor: "Louise, Louise are you alright Louise."

Louise: "Daddy help please, he's trying to get in." Then there was a sizzling sound coming from the phone and the signal cut out.

Elaine: "What's wrong? Is Louise alright?"

Connor: "Yes she's fine, the phone just went dead."

And then just by luck the reporter on the television said that the phone services had cut out along with the mobile phones. Apparently the system had overloaded and people were asked to stay indoors until this crisis is over.

Connor: I'm going to get Louise but first we need to make sure that this place is locked up tighter than a drum. Elaine check upstairs and I'll sort down here."

Elaine: "I bet your glad now that I got all the extra security in this place. You can't call me paranoid now."

Connor: "You're right, I can't. You were spot on now, go on go upstairs and lock everything up."

It only took a few minutes to secure the house and Elaine run down the stairs.

Elaine: "There are some zombies on the street, how are you going to get to Louise now?"

I turned off the light and went to the living room window and looked out on to the street.

Connor: "There aren't that many and they're pretty spread out, I could get away quietly enough without drawing too much attention to myself. Turn off all the lights, I'll be back as soon as I can. Get Dominic and Sara down into the living room where you can keep an eye on them and stay as quiet as possible. I love you sweetheart."

I went to my workshop in the backyard and picked up a crowbar from the workbench and went back into the house.

I opened the front door slowly. The coast was clear. As I headed to the car Elaine closed and locked the front door to the house.

I managed to get into my car without detection then I let the hand brake off and the car rolled out of the driveway and down the street none of the zombies seemed to be agitated in any way.

The car stopped at the bottom of the street, I sat up straight and turned the key in the ignition. Then two of the zombies looked at me and started to run in my direction, screaming wildly. Then I realised that sound was definitely attracting them.

This alerted others to where I was and before I knew it there were dozens of them running and screaming like wild beasts towards my car. I turned the key again the car started I sped away.

I drove straight to the street that Louise's friend June lived on. The place was teaming with those things, how the hell was I going to get to June's house?

I decided to leave the car and try to get there on foot by going through from the back of the houses so I got out of the car slowly and quietly and bolted to the gable end house at the bottom of June's row.

I prayed that none of the things saw me. I also prayed that Louise was alright and that I was in time.

I was in luck, there was a direct pathway to June's house at the back of the row of houses there didn't seem to be any zombies but I knew I still had to be careful.

I hopped over the first fence, then the second and third, so far so good. There were no zombies, everything seemed to be clear and I decided to take a straight run to the back door of June's house.

I got to the last fence and just as I was about to jump over it I heard a blood-curdling scream coming from the house beside me. I scrambled to the side of the French doors and looked into the living room. There was a woman being eaten by a man and what looked like a five or six-year-old girl who must have been her daughter.

They were tearing the flesh from the woman's body like animals and what was worse was that she seemed to be still alive. Her eyes were moving and with each bite the man and little girl took the blood which spurted from the wounds on her body.

The sight I witnessed sickened me to the core but I knew that there was nothing I could do for her. As I turned to jump over the fence my foot knocked over a plant pot and it smashed I dived over the fence and hid in a dark part of the garden.

Suddenly a zombie came crashing through the French window. It looked around and there were large shards of glass from the window protruding from it's face and head. Then to my horror it seemed to look over in my direction and I could swear that it had seen me but a few seconds later it turned away and grunted then shuffled back into the house.

I was terrified. It took all my willpower to get moving again. I went to the back door and tried the door handle. The door opened and I walked in then closed it behind me.

I took the crowbar from the back of my belt and held it tight, then slowly but carefully started to look around. I remembered that she said she was in the attic so I headed upstairs and half way up I heard groaning.

The landing was poorly lit but it was bright enough to see a zombie standing at the attic door. I stepped quietly up the rest of the stairs and the zombie swung around and came towards me screaming.

With one swing of my crowbar I hit him on the head. He stopped, then staggered backwards as his eyes turned inwards and he dropped to the ground.

I walked to the attic door and put my ear to it. I couldn't hear anything. Then I called out Louise's name and then I could hear her calling for me and things being moved from the door. The next thing I knew was Louise jumping into my arms crying and saying my name over and over again.

Connor: "Calm down love, daddy's here now, who's with you?"

Louise: "Come on out," she shouted. "This is my friend June, her mom Mary and her Uncle Tim."

Mary and June looked over at the dead man on the floor and they both started to cry. I realised that it was Mary's husband, June's father.

Connor: "Are any of you hurt?"

Mary: "Yes I was, my husband Paul, bit a piece of my arm off."

Connor: "It doesn't seem too bad we can get a more permanent dressing on that when we get back to my place."

Mary: "Why your place? Where we are is just as good isn't it?"

Connor: "This house is too unprotected. Thanks to my wife my house is somewhat like the Tower of London, no one can get into it without the keys. Now what will it be? Make up your mind because Louise and me are going."

Mary: "Ok we're coming, where's your car?"

Connor: "Well there's a small problem there. I had to leave the car at the bottom of the road and I had to come the back way over the fences and through the back door."

Mary: "So how the hell do we get out of here then?"

Connor: "We go the same way I came and if we stay relatively quiet we'll all get to my house in one piece."

Mary and the others agreed. I looked out of the front window and it seemed that there were more zombies than when I had got here at the start.

Then we headed to the back door, I opened it quietly and looked out.

The zombie from next door spotted me and it started to scream loudly with a high-pitched tone. A few seconds later I could see in the distance zombies running up the way I had come in.

I slammed the door and locked it. Almost immediately a group of those things started to pound on the door.

Connor: "It won't take long for them to get in we need another way out."

June: "What about dad's car Mum, we can take that?"

Mary: "It's out on the driveway and I'm not going to get it."

Connor: "You don't have to, where's the keys?"

June: "it's in dad's pocket."

Tim: "I'll get them, I won't be long."

I started to tap the walls around the front of the house it was all done in breezeblock there was no way I could back the car through this part of the house.

Mary: "What are you doing?" she asked with a bewildered look on her face.

Connor: "Only one of us can go for the car, it's safer. I have to find a soft place in the brick so I can get the back of the car through and get the rest of you into the car safely but unfortunately I'll never be able get the car through this it's too strong and the back of the house is too narrow.

Mary: "What about the garage? There's a door over there that leads into it, my husband had it built six months ago."

Tim came down the stairs with the keys in his hand. I took them and put them into my pocket then I entered the garage to make sure that it was all clear.

Connor: "Ok get yourselves a weapon and stand ready at the opening of the door. When I come through the garage door with the car get in as quickly as possible then we can get the hell out of here. Now, do you all understand?" Everyone agreed on the plan.

I went to the front door and put my hand on the handle. Louise came over to me and wrapped her arms around my neck and squeezed, then she smiled at me. I smiled back and told her everything was going to be alright. I took a few deep breaths and opened the door.

When I got outside I closed the door behind me. It made a small noise as I closed it and I dived behind the car with my breath held. I took a quick look from where I was sitting but none of them were alerted.

I crept around to the driver side and put the key into the car door. When I turned it the alarm let out two loud beeps and one of the zombies looked in my direction. I knew my luck wouldn't hold so I got up and into the car quickly and locked the doors. In a few seconds the car was surrounded, I started it up and put the accelerator to the floor. I drove the car out into the street then I put it into reverse and backed it through the garage doors.

Louise shouted "Come on," and they piled into the back of the car. I pressed the accelerator hard and drove away knocking down several zombies.

It took about twenty minutes to get back home and the street was still relatively quiet but there were some zombies shuffling about.

Connor: "I'm going to drive up to the house and when I stop I'll get out first, the rest of you get out and head to the house. Louise shout for your mommy and when she opens the door get in as fast as you can."

When I got out the rest ran to the door and when Louise shouted Elaine opened the door. Two of the zombies ran towards me but I swung the crowbar in their direction.

When I hit the first one he flew back and knocked the other onto the ground, then I turned and ran towards the house. I got in then closed and locked the door.

As Elaine hugged me I noticed that there were a lot of people from the street in the house. I asked Elaine where all these people had come from.

Elaine: "When the zombies started to appear on the street they all started to panic as they were running away in their cars. The ones that had no transport didn't seem to know what to do so I got them in here with us. I hope that's alright."

Connor: "That's fine I suppose."

But what I was thinking was far from what I had said. I knew we couldn't stay here forever. It would have been hard enough to get my own family to relative safety but how was I going to get all these people to safety if the situation got worse.

Suddenly we heard a scream coming from the kitchen. I ran in and June's mother had passed out but Elaine went to Mary's assistance. June's blood was running out of her arm, Elaine woke her up and started to clean treat her wound.

Elaine: "What happened to your arm Mary?"

Mary: "I hurt it earlier, I'm sorry about this I don't do this sort of thing very often, I just don't feel very well I think my ulcers are flaring up again."

I got everybody into the living room then I asked for quiet.

Connor: "We have a problem we can't stay here for any length of time and I didn't expect so many people to be here so we're going to have to come up with some sort of ideas of how we're going to get everybody out of here and where we are going to go."

A man put up his hand I looked at him he said that he was Brian Reel.

Brian: "Surly the police and the army must be sorting things out."

Connor: "I don't know Brian, we'll have to wait and see."

Elaine turned on the television, the reporter said that our country wasn't the only one that this was happening to, according to him it was happening all over the world and it seemed that no one knew what was going on.

It was widely blamed on some sort of virus but there was no confirmation from any government origination to be truthful and I don't think anybody anywhere knew what was going on or how it was to be stopped.

Later that night everybody was asleep but I sat at the television hoping to god that someone could figure out what was going on or at least give a list of where we could go if there was an evacuation.

There were reports on some countries sending out what they called 'kill squads' and a country in Europe had nuked another country to try to stop the spread of whatever this was.

Every country in the world was blaming each other for spreading a virus. Different religions for once were agreed, it was the rapture the end of days. The way they were talking you'd think the four horsemen of the apocalypse were going to ride out of the sky at any moment. The whole planet was in a panic.

In this country no one in the government, the police or even the army knew what was going on until it was too late. I just hoped that for all our sakes they managed to start sorting out this whole mess.

Suddenly the station went off the air without warning and then a message appeared on the screen it was the emergency frequency. I frantically turned to each channel, but each and every one was the same. It was then I knew we were in deep trouble.

I sat on the floor, then turned off the television and sobbed quietly. I must of fallen asleep because when I opened my eyes it was bright and my wife had her hand on my shoulder. For a moment I thought it was a really bad dream until Elaine spoke.

Elaine: "There's something wrong with Mary, she's running a high temperature and I think the wound on her arm is infected. I gave her a large dose of antibiotics early this morning but nothing's working. She's just getting worse if we can't lower her temperature she'll start having seizures and then she'll die."

Connor: "I'll go have a look at her."

June started to shout for Elaine and we ran upstairs. Mary was lying still. Elaine checked her pulse.

Elaine: "I'm sorry June, she's gone," she said with a tremor in her voice.

June with a stunned look on her face started to scream and cry. Louise grabbed her and comforted her and she took June to her room so she could calm her down.

A few minutes later June came from Louise's room and said that she was going to sit in the garden for a while but I didn't worry about it as the back garden was well blocked off with a large wall.

I was about to talk to Elaine when I heard a moan. I slowly looked over to the bed and Mary's body started to move. I backed up to the set of drawers behind me, put my hand up and grabbed a large wooden ornament.

Mary suddenly bounced out of the bed and went straight for Elaine. Mary grabbed her by the hair and pulled her head back and with her mouth wide open she went to bite Elaine on the neck.

I ran over and raised the wooden ornament then I thrust it down on the back of Mary's head as hard as I could, the ornament broke.

She turned and attacked me. She tried to rip my face off but as she was struggling with me Elaine lifted the broken ornament and stabbed Mary in through the back of the head.

Mary's body fell to the floor and this time she wasn't getting back up again. It was then I knew that to keep these things down we had to do massive damage to the brain.

Connor: "Let's get the body back on the bed, I don't want June to see her mother like this. Come on Elaine let's go. What's wrong?"

Elaine: "Do you know what this means? That if any of us are bitten or gets bitten we're going to be infected with whatever this is and it puts us all in danger. We have to check everyone and if anyone has been infected we have to quarantine them."

Connor: "They all seem healthy enough."

Elaine: "It's better to be safe than sorry."

We went downstairs and explained what happened in the bedroom with June's mother a few minutes earlier and what we thought was the cause.

Elaine: "I'll set up an examination area over there and I'll look at each of you one at time. Ok let's get started."

Brian: "I don't want to sound ignorant but what gives you the authority to examine any of us. It should be someone from the medical profession that should do it.

Connor: "It's ok Brian, Elaine was a fully qualified nurse. She took a break from nursing a couple of years ago to be with the kids more."

Elaine: "And because this is my house, you're first Brian," then she winked and everybody laughed as she seemed to put them all at ease.

Connor: "Louise, go and get June we need to tell her what's going on."

It wasn't long before Louise came running into the living room in a panic and crying, "She's killed herself dad," she screamed. Elaine and I ran out to the backyard and to see what June had done. She had cut deep into her wrists and bled to death. We carried her up the stairs and laid her body beside her mother's and closed the door.

Later that day I walked over to Dominic and Sara and knelt down.

Connor: "How are you holding up big man?"

Dominic: "Ok dad, but I'm a little frightened."

Conner: "It's alright to be scared Dominic, we're all a little scared, don't worry son. And what about my little girl are you alright love."

Sara: "Yes daddy, I'm not scared. If one of those bad men comes in here I'll fight him," she said with a determined look on her face.

I laughed and rubbed her little head. A few minutes later Mat from down the road turned the television on.

Mat: "Is the dish still working I can't seem to get a station."

Connor: "There's nothing wrong with the dish it's the emergency frequency."

Mat: "Were there any evacuation details?"

Connor: "No, one minute the news was on the next this."

Brian: "What does it mean?"

Mat: "It means that we're screwed."

Brian: "Help has to be coming what would you know about it any way?"

Mat: "I was in the army for eighteen years. The last three black ops kind of stuff we were given training on matters of this magnitude like the people that they save first and foremost are the top-ranking people in government top scientists and their families."

Brian: "What you're saying is the government knew about this before it was going to happen."

Mat: "No, not this, nuclear holocaust and things like that. I doubt if anyone saw this coming. I think Connor was right, we should find a way out of here and get to a more secure area. It's our only chance of survival."

Connor: "Mat's right. Just before the television went off last night it showed pictures from all over the world. The whole planet's got the same problem so we should get used to being on our own. I've been thinking about this, on our way back last night there was an abandoned bus big enough to carry us all and more if we meet up with more survivors on the way."

Dominic: "If we do get out of here where do we go?"

Brian: "That's a smart boy you have there Connor, he's right, where are we going to go?"

Connor: About five miles out of town there's a recently disused police station with weapons and plenty of cover. The station is well penned in, we'll be safe and armed."

Mat: "How do you know this?"

Connor: "I work for the company that has been contracted to disarm and disassemble."

Brian: "How do you know the place hasn't been raided or taken over?"

Connor: "I don't but it may be the only chance we have, I say take it, but we all need to agree."

Mat: "Why is this police station so far outside town it doesn't seem like it was a police station to me."

Connor: "Strictly speaking it wasn't, it was more a storage house for illegal guns, pipe bombs and other paraphernalia that were seized."

Elaine: "It would be dangerous, and I'm not talking about the zombies, there must be guards and if there is, they'll be armed."

Connor: "You're right there were guards posted but not in the compound outside. The place is locked up tighter than a swan's ass and I know where the keys are, at my office. I have automatic access and the men that were guarding the place are either dead or they have run off. The only risk we will take is getting the key."

Mat: "I'm with you."

Brian: "Yep so am I at this point we have nothing to lose let's do it."

Everybody agreed so then we put our heads together and made a plan.

The first part of the plan was to get the abandoned bus and drive it back here without doing too much damage to it then pick up all survivors.

The second part of the plan was that we drive to my office and get the keys for the police compound the and third part was that we got our ass's and any survivors we met on the way to the compound then maybe we would be safe.

Connor: "Ok who knows how to drive a bus?" I looked around, only one knew how.

Connor: "So there's only Mat and me. Right, does anybody know how to hotwire a bus just in case the keys are gone?"

Mat: "I do, the army gives you many skills."

Elaine: "You would be as well waiting till dark, but in the meantime, we all have to arm ourselves."

A couple of hours later when darkness fell, Mat and me headed for the car outside the house. There still weren't many zombies about which was in our favour. We got into the car and let the handbrake off and like before the car rolled down the hill silently.

At the bottom of the hill I started the engine but I kept the lights off and drove slowly so as not to attract attention from those things.

A little while later we came across the bus. We got out of the car and edged our way slowly over to the bus doors which were open so we quietly got in and carefully closed the doors.

Mat: "The keys are in the ignition, now the moment of truth."

Mat turned the key it started first time.

Mat: "The luck was with us thanks be to god."

Connor: "What about the fuel?"

Mat: "She's full. Ok we're on our way."

We drove to the bottom of my street and there were a few more zombies there but Mat started up the engine and kept sounding the horn.

Connor: "What are you doing, are you mad?"

Mat: "Nope, we'll lure as many of them down here, then we speed up, stop outside the house and it gives everybody a better chance to get into the bus without getting hurt."

It took a while but at least four dozen of them were beating on the bus, before Mat raced up to the house. I got out and Elaine came out with all the kids that were there, then the women. It only took a few minutes to load everybody into the bus.

Mat drove to my office and he pulled up tight to the main doors as planed. Everybody hid in the bus and waited till the zombies cleared away. "I need a few people to come with me just in case I need help."

Tim: "I'll go, it's better than sitting here not knowing whether you got the key or got killed."

Mat: "I'll go."

Connor: "No, you'll have to stay. You're the only one other than me who knows how to drive this thing. If anything happens to me you have to get these people to safety."

Brian: "Ah crap, I'll go."

Mat: "How will I know if you're alright or not?"

Connor: "I'll go and get a couple of radios out of the guard station."

A few minutes later I came back with a walkie-talkie.

Connor: "They're working I checked them out. If there's any problem contact me straight away other than that don't make a sound. I'll contact you every step of the way."

Connor: "Ok, Tim, Brian, we're ready to go. Remember keep your weapons up, stick together, don't make any sudden moves and above all stay quiet, they seem to be attracted by sound. Let's go."

Brian, Tim and I walked into the foyer, it seemed to be free of zombies.

Tim: "Do we take the elevator or the stairwell?"

Brian: "It might be better to take the stairs, the elevator makes that dinging sound it might attract some unwanted attention."

Connor: "You're probably right, we'd be better taking the stairs."

Tim: "But the elevator would be quicker that's what we want, to get in and out as fast as possible."

Connor: "You're right too but we want to get out in one piece."

We headed towards the entrance to the stairwell and I opened the door. The stairs were empty we walked slowly and quietly till we got to the fourteenth floor where my office was located I took the walky-talky out of my pocket.

Connor: "Mat, are you there? Is everything alright?"

Mat: "Yep I'm here. Things seem to be alright, what's it like on your side?"

Connor: "We're on the stairwell outside the floor where my office is. We're about to enter so we won't be contacting you till we're on the way out, so remember get ready to get that thing going the moment you see us."

Mat: "Good luck and be careful."

Tim opened the door leading onto the floor were my office was. It seemed to be deserted so we walked down the long dark hallway it only took a few minutes to get to my office. I took my key card from my coat pocket and swiped it. My office door unlocked.

Connor: "You two stay here, I'll go and get the security card for the vault."

I went to my desk and activated the computer. I put my secret code into the computer along with a scan of my thumbprint and a picture on the wall moved to one side automatically.

Behind it there was a small safe. I punched in the combination, the small safe door opened and inside there was a gold coloured security pass card.

I went and opened the door of my office then Brian, Tim and I walked down the corridor. At the end was a large steel door. I took the pass card and swiped it, but nothing happened, I swiped it again still nothing.

Tim: "What's wrong, is the card broken?"

Connor: "No, sometimes a new card can take a few goes to work."

Tim: "We don't have the time we need to get in now."

Connor: "Calm down and be patent, it'll work now, shut up."

I swiped it again, the green light suddenly came on then the door opened. We walked into the vault and at the side of the room was a group of my work mates.

Connor: "What are you all doing here?"

Jerry: "O'Brian it's only you what are you doing here? You can't come in this is our place."

Connor: "Don't worry Jerry, I'm not staying, we're just here to get something we need."

Jerry: "What would you need here, there is nothing here that belongs to you O'Brian. Where did you get that pass card? You stole it didn't you? When this is all over I'll see you in jail," he said with a hint of gratification in his voice.

Connor: "It's my pass card Jerry, look my name is on it."

Jerry: "It's a fake, it has to be, that's the pass key to the restricted section."

Connor: "That's right, Dawson gave it to me a week ago he put me in charge of the station one deconstruction project."

Jerry: "So you're going to be my boss soon, well at the minute I'm still yours and you brought unauthorised people into the vault, you're fired and when this is all sorted out I'll make sure you get prosecuted to the full extent of the law."

Connor: "For Christ sake Jerry, wise up. There's no help coming. Whatever is happening is happening everywhere and we're on our own Jerry. Now don't be a dick and get out of my way."

Jerry stepped out of the way, I went to the restricted section of the vault and opened the drawer with the pass card. I looked inside the drawer there was a key, I took it and put it in my jacket.

Brian: "is that what we came for? That's it? Mat could have picked the lock, it would have been easier and faster."

Connor: "Mat couldn't pick the lock that this key fits."

Tim: "Why not?"

Connor: "Because this key and the lock that comes with it are hardened titanium. The key is fingerprint protected and only I can use it. There are only four keys."

Tim: "What about the holders of the other three keys, maybe they had the same idea."

"I doubt it, the people that have them are in the city, coming here would be the last thing on their mind."

Brian: "Someone could have climbed over the fencing and opened it somehow from the other side."

Connor: "When the place is locked the outer walls are automatically electrified – well except for a small area round the chain and lock. Listen to me everybody, we've got a bus outside we're going somewhere safe, I hope. I'm not too sure whether it is or not but it's our only hope. All of you are welcome if you want to come, say now."

They all put their hands up I counted seven women and eight men not including Jerry.

Connor: "What do you say Jerry, are you in or not."

Jerry: "You can't take them, they'll get ripped apart by them things out there."

Connor: "I don't like you Jerry but I would never forgive myself if I left you here on your own so it's your choice you can stay here on your own but if the zombies don't get you you'll starve to death so what will it be?"

Jerry: "Ok I'll come," he said with anger in his voice.

Tim took the lead as we all walked down the corridor when Tim got to the door that lead to the stairwell he shouted, "It's all clear."

Brian: "Shut up for god sake, they'll hear you."

Tim: "It's ok, there's none of them here."

Suddenly two zombies came screaming out of one of the offices and grabbed Tim they dragged him to the ground and started to rip out his flesh with their teeth he was screaming for us to help him.

One of the women started to scream O MY GOOD GOD WE'RE ALL GOING TO DIE I went to help Tim but Brian pulled me back.

Brian: "It's too late for him, we have to get going."

I stood there with a look of horror. I was stunned, Brian grabbed me by the arm.

Brian: "Come on for Christ sake, snap out of it and run everyone, run for the stairwell door, hurry," he roared.

We all got through the door and I looked down the stairs. As far as I could see there were no more of them. I took the walkie-talkie out of my jacket.

Connor: "Mat are you still there?"

Mat: "Yes is everybody alright?"

Connor: "No they got Tim. He's dead, they ate him alive, literally, but the rest of us are ok. Is everything alright down there?"

Mat: "No problems here Connor, did you get the key?"

Connor: "Yes I got it and we also found some more survivors."

Mat: "The more the merrier, hurry up we have to go."

We ran down the stairs and got out of the door into the foyer. There were no zombies. As we approached the bus Mat started it up and we could hear the zombies screaming and beating the side of the bus. They were in a frenzy as we got to the open doors of the bus and hurriedly got in. Mat closed the doors behind us then we pulled off. We drove through the streets and it was sad to see how quickly the human race broke down.

I thought to myself, so this is the legacy we leave or kids. At that moment I was ashamed, all I wanted to do was break down and cry. I looked over at my kids, maybe we still have a chance, maybe we can rebuild.

It took us about an hour to get to the station. Mat stopped outside the police compound everything seemed to be quiet.

Mat: "Give me the key, it's my turn to do something."

Connor: "You can't, the key is coded to my finger prints but I need someone to watch my back, you want to come with me?"

Mat: "I'm there, lead the way."

Connor: "What about you Jerry? Want to help?"

I saw the look of fear in his face so I told him to stay and look after the people on the bus so he wouldn't look like a fool in front of everybody. I could see he was almost overwhelmed with relief.

I told Mat to open the doors, then we got out and I walked over to the lock I took the key out of my pocket and put it in the lock then I turned the key praying that it was programmed with my fingerprint.

I heard a clicking sound the lock opened and I let out a sigh of relief.

Connor: "Go back to the bus and get ready to drive her through and tell Brian to give me a hand with the gate."

Mat nodded his head and walked back to the bus. A few seconds later Brian came up to the gates and helped me open them up. Mat drove the bus in as quiet as he could.

When the bus was all the way into the compound Brian and I closed the gates and locked them with the large bolt that was attached to the back of the gates.

This was my first time here it was a large compound with a high steel wall-like barrier around it. Inside there were two large buildings, I remember from the plans the main building was the living quarters for the personnel.

The back building was where they stored the weapons the outer compound seemed to be secured. I walked over to the bus Mat opened the door.

Connor: "Come with us Mat we need your expertise. You were in the army, we'll need to track the weapons. Everybody stay put and keep the door closed till we give the all clear.

Brian, Mat and I went to the large building at the back and Mat got there first.

Mat: "It's locked with the same sort of lock that was on the main gate, we're screwed."

Connor: "This key will open all locks in this place, it's a master key when we unlock the locks we'll leave them off."

We walked into the building and Brian searched for the light. When he found it he threw the switch and the whole place lit up like a Christmas tree. I looked over at Mat I could see the joy on his face.

Connor: "Go and get something quick and easy to use for the three of us then we'll search the rest of the place."

Mat ran off through the warehouse like a child in a sweet shop and about ten minutes later he came back with three pump action shot guns and a few boxes of shells.

Mat: "These things are easy to use. All you have to do is slip the shells in here. It takes eight shots every time. You shoot, cock like this and fire again. It has a wide dispersal range and kicks like a bad tempered horse so hold it tight to your shoulder. Oh and watch that none of us is in the way, now let's get to it it's getting dark."

It took about two and a half hours for the three of us to search the whole compound it was pitch dark when we had finished.

We went back to the bus and started to unload everybody and get them into the building that was used as living quarters then we got everybody settled.

It was the first time in two days that we all could relax; people were actually laughing and joking. Over the next few hours I noticed that Jerry was following Elaine about like a lap dog.

He always had a thing about her, it didn't bother me until now but I put it out of my mind mainly because I knew he freaked Elaine out but I did know because of the situation we were all in that I would have to keep an eye on him.

I decided to rescue Elaine and walked over to her. Jerry looked at me and smiled then he walked away.

Connor: "Are you alright Elaine?"

Elaine: "I'm alright love, it's just Jerry, he's acting weird, smiling at me, touching my arm, helping me, you know just weird."

Connor: "I think in his own way he's just trying to be helpful."

Elaine: "But I'm the only one he's helping I think he thinks something might happen between us the whole thing is starting to make me uncomfortable.

Connor: "Look I'll keep an eye on him and if he does something wrong I'll speak to him."

Then she threw her arms around me and gave me a kiss and told me that she loved me. I made sure that Louise, Dominic and Sara were alright and kissed them good night.

The next morning we broke up into groups one group checked food and medical supplies the other checked the armoury and later that day we got together and talked about our situation.

Brian: "Ok, let's start, first off I want to know who is leading our little band, we need a chain of command. Does anybody want to put themselves forward for this?"

Jerry: "I do, I have years of experience in the area of leadership."

Connor: "What a surprise, I didn't see that one coming."

Jerry: "If you aren't going to bring something constructive to the table leave the room," He said with a smug expression.

Connor: "I'll put Mat forward to be the boss."

Jerry: "He's just being petty, I am the man for this job not a soldier. We are civilians after all not soldiers."

Connor: "No, what we need is someone that can get us ready for battle if needs be, not a self-loathing bully with a Hitler complex."

Jerry: "How dare you talk about me that way? Ladies and gentlemen what we need is leadership and I'm the leader we need to get us through these trying times."

Mat: "People, I'm flattered by Connor's proposal but I don't want to be a leader, I can train people with all the weapons, I don't need leadership to do that."

Jerry: "So it's settled. I'm to lead our merry bunch. Good. The first thing were going to do is..."

Brian: "Hold it, I put Connor's name forward."

Jerry: "Are you crazy? He doesn't have a clue, he has no experience."

Brian: "For someone with no experience he did quite well on his first time out he and his wife took most of us in when this whole thing started, they didn't just think of themselves, and remember Connor thought of the plan to get us all here and he didn't shy away from carrying it out. He got us here, and he should be the one to carry on."

Jerry: "What about the man he got killed back at the office, he froze."

Mat: "I was there people, poor Tim got himself killed, and as we know once you get bitten sooner or later it's over."

Brian: "What you're talking about is cowardice let's talk about that Jerry. When we entered the vault you were the one hiding in the corner behind all the women. I suggest we vote."

Brian looked around and counted the show of hands for Jerry and me. I won. Jerry wasn't too pleased but he kept his composure.

Connor: "What's the situation with the guns?"

Mat: "We have enough guns and ammo to last a lifetime."

Elaine: "The problem is the food and medical supplies. We don't have much of either."

Connor: "We need to get into town somehow to stock up on supplies, the bus won't do the job, we need something that runs better."

Mat: "If it helps, I found three old armoured trucks. They're not working at the moment but I may be able to get at least one running and I found a short wave radio, I could maybe boost the signal to take in a wider range we might pick up some more survivors."

Jerry: "Are you people crazy? We can't go back out there, and we can't bring any more people in here, what if there infected? All our lives could be put in danger."

Connor: "Maybe, but we do need supplies and the only way of getting them is to go outside. We'll vote on it."

I looked around and most agreed to go back outside to get survivors and supplies.

Over the next week, Mat started on the trucks and the radio and we also started to train with the weapons. At the end of the week Mat got two of the trucks working. Finally, the day came when we were to go on our first supplies run. The task was down to Brian, Mat and myself.

We drove out of the compound at daybreak and went back to town. The place was full of zombies but we managed to stock the trucks with all the supplies we needed with relative ease and without incident.

When we got back we saw a car outside the compound. We drove up behind the car and Mat sounded the horn and the gates opened up and the people in the car drove in.

We followed. I looked out of the back of the truck and I noticed on the road behind us there were some zombies. I knew that it wouldn't take long for them to realise that we were in the compound and having that car outside the gates didn't help.

When the gates were closed and secured I got out of the truck and spoke to Elaine.

Connor: "Elaine why didn't you let the car in when it arrived?"

Elaine: "I had nothing to do with it, Jerry wouldn't let us open the gates, he was worried about infection. Since you left he's been strutting about like king of the walk. I got the impression that he hoped that you wouldn't make it, I think it would have made his day. Please Connor, watch your back."

Jerry came over as I was talking to Elaine.

Connor: "Did you stop Elaine and the others from letting that car in?"

Jerry: "Yes we can't just let anyone in, you put me in charge while you were away, I used my discretion."

Connor: "By using your discretion you may have alerted the zombies of our presence."

Jerry: "They were going to find out anyway so what's the problem?"

Connor: "The problem is it's going to be much harder to get in or out if we need supplies or if we can get in touch with any more survivors we won't be able to let them in without letting a bunch of those things in to the compound as well. This will be the last time I leave you in charge Jerry but we'll keep this to ourselves."

A meeting was called that night to talk about our situation.

Elaine: "We have more than enough food and medical supplies."

Connor: "What about fuel for the trucks?"

Brian: "The storage tank at the back of the compound is about three quarters full. We'll be fine for a long time if the electrics hold out and we don't have to use the generator. I also think I can bypass the safety to electrify the fences again."

Conner: "Can you do it without blowing us all up?"

Brian: "Yes, but it'll take time. The walls on the inside are insulated by concrete so no one can get harmed on the inside but we have to insulate the inside of the gate. I may also be able to get the automatic bolt release operational again."

Connor: "We may have a bigger problem. Those things outside are starting to gather, soon we won't be able to get out of here without letting some of them in and I'm sure you'll agree we can't let that happen."

Mat: "I've been working on that. Just in case we could build a barrier around the gates, a square box big enough to hold three to four large trucks. Then we can have a place for a couple of people on top with guns."

Brian: "How would it work?"

Mat: "We build a structure each side of the gates then build a double gate to close off the gaps. We drive the vehicles in, close the first set of gates, if Brian can get the automatic locking device working, then all we have to do is open the outside gates. The vehicles can then drive on. All we have to do is press a button, the outside gates close and the zombies that are hemmed in get taken out by the people on the top with guns and when the trucks come back we do the same thing."

Connor: "So this plan sort of hinges on Brian getting the automatic system on the gates working?"

Mat: "Yes but even if he doesn't get it working we could maybe rig something up to do the same job."

Connor: "What would you need to make this work?"

Mat: "All the materials I need are here. All I need is everybody to help and the quicker we get to it the quicker we'll finish it."

Connor: "Ok we'll start tomorrow. Oh Elaine, how are our new guests doing?"

Elaine: "There are three men and one woman. The girl Kate has a broken leg. I checked them for infection they're clean."

Connor: "Good, who are the men?"

Elaine: "I don't know much about them but their names are Peter, John and Carl."

Connor: "Will you tell them about the plan and that we are going to need their help with the building of the new wall and gates."

Elaine: "Ok I'll do it now."

About a half an hour later, out in the compound Elaine called me over.

Connor: "What's wrong Elaine?"

Elaine: "It's those new men, they're refusing to help with anything. You'll have to talk to them, they won't listen to me."

I went in to the main building. John, Peter and Carl were sitting around a table talking. I walked over to the table.

Connor: "Hello gentlemen, I'm Conner."

Peter: "Hello Connor, I don't care," he said while laughing.

Connor: "Elaine tells me you refuse to help out."

John: "Who's Elaine? Oh yes, that sexy bit of stuff that spoke to us when we got here, you remember Peter."

Carl: "Yes Mmmm I wouldn't mind working on her for a while but that's all the work we'll be doing."

They sat there and started to laugh. I could feel my temper raising, I clenched my fist and hit Carl in the face.

Connor: "Now listen to me, you pieces of crap, we aren't asking you to help around here we're telling you."

Peter: "What if we don't do as you tell us."

Connor: "Then you can go back were you've come from."

John: "You could live with yourself turning us back out in the streets to get eaten by those things."

Connor: "If you won't do as you're told then I'll gladly send you out to those things."

Carl: "Ok we'll do as we're told."

I walked away but something didn't seem right about them. When I got outside into the compound I spotted Jerry and I called him over.

Jerry: "What can I do for you?"

Connor: "I'm beginning to think you were right about some of the people in that car."

Jerry: "How was I right?"

Connor: "There's something about them I don't trust, I want you to befriend them, it's very important you gain their trust. We need to know what their up to."

Jerry: "How do you propose I do that?"

Connor: "They don't seem to like me, play on that, say you don't like me, that should give you an excuse."

Jerry: "But I don't like you."

Connor: "Then it should be easy. Oh that reminds me touch or even look at my wife in the wrong way again and I'll bitch slap you in front of everyone. Ok? Do we understand each other?"

Jerry: "Oh we understand each other," he said with a soft angry tone.

I knew when I said that I was going to have trouble somewhere along the line. After that night Jerry started to openly disagree with every plan I had come up with, at first I thought he was playing a part for Carl and his friends but after a while I wasn't too sure.

Over the next month the work went slowly but at last it was finished and surprisingly it worked. We started to pick up stranded survivors that we heard over the short wave radio that Mat had set up.

With all the people that we picked up and the people that started to arrive we needed a lot more supplies. I knew sooner or later we would have to make another supply run.

I thought of taking Jerry this time but I just couldn't trust him not to freeze at the moment we would most need him and he's useless. I asked him to keep an eye on Carl and his friends but he couldn't even do that so I decided to take Brian, Peter and Mat with me.

We got our guns and got the two trucks and drove to the town centre then went round at full speed at the back of the large store on the main street.

Mat got out of the truck with a circular saw and cut the locked door. We could hear the zombies' high-pitched screams coming our way. Mat swung the doors open and the rest of us drove the trucks into the delivery yard at the back of the store.

Mat took the saw and snapped the lock on the back entrance of the store.

Connor: "Mat, you and Brian get the food, Peter and myself will sort out the medical supplies. We'll meet back at the trucks in twenty minutes, lets go."

Peter and I got the medical supplies together we left them at the door then we went back to see if there was something else we needed I was looking in the cabinets when I heard Peter say.

Peter: "Turn around slowly, you prick," he said smugly.

Connor: "So Carl hasn't got the balls to do his own dirty work himself."

Peter: "Carl didn't tell me to do this, Jerry did. We'll be better off with him in charge. You shouldn't have pissed with him. Oh and bye bye."

All I could hear was the gun going off and I felt an excruciating pain in my head. I remember falling to the ground and watching Peter fire two shots into the air then he ran shouting, "They got him, the bastards got Connor."

Then I started to drift away, I knew it was over for me, the only thing I regretted was that I would be leaving Elaine, Dominic and Sara behind then everything went black.

I opened my eyes. I was in a hospital bed. I pulled out the drip that was in my arm and walked to the mirror. I was weak but I was still alive.

My face was scarred but there was something wrong, it didn't look quite like me. I stumbled to the door of the room and opened it. A man came running towards me he was shouting for the doctor.

He told me that I had to get back into bed and he helped me back. A few second later another man walked in and he introduced himself as Doctor Morgan.

Doctor Morgan: "I thought you would never wake up, let's have a look at you, yes, you've healed well."

Connor: "Where am I and how long was I out?"

Doctor Morgan: "You're in a hospital you've been in a coma for three months. You're lucky my people were in the store looking for supplies. They thought you were dead until one of them noticed you twitching and checked your pulse they brought you back with them."

Connor: "My face doctor, what happened to my face?"

Doctor Morgan: "There was a lot of damage done to the soft tissue of the face we had to do a lot of reconstructive surgery but it didn't turn out too badly.

Connor: "Where is this place? There doesn't seem to be any zombie activity."

Doctor: "We're on an abandoned oil rig. We've been here for almost five years. It's nothing special but we made it our own. We have almost everything here we decided to make a community of our own away from the hustle and bustle of everyday life. It's far from perfect but we do try. We needed to get out of main stream life. No one noticed a bunch of doctors just left. Most people thought we were mad. Now what happened to you?"

Connor: "A group of my men turned on me so they could take over the compound to be the boss. I didn't think they would have had the balls to do this but they showed me didn't they?"

Doctor: "You're welcome to stay with us for as long as you like."

Connor: "It's an offer I would normally take, but I have a family back there and I have to go get them."

Doctor: "You are welcome to return with your family and anyone else who would want to come with you."

"Thanks Doctor Morgan I might take you up on that offer."

"But first we need to get you to full strength."

There was one thing I thought was strange about these people. There didn't seem to be any women or children. Maybe that's why Doctor Morgan extended the invitation to bring back as many people as I liked.

It took me a month and a half to get myself ready. During that time Doctor Morgan and I talked often. Apparently the reason these people left society was because they knew that there was going to be a worldwide epidemic. He told me they didn't know what form it would take.

I asked him why they did not try to warn the governments of the world of this disaster. If they had, all this may have been avoided. He told me they did warn the appropriate authorities but they were branded madmen and released from their contracts. They were shunned in the scientific communities. I asked him how they found out about this epidemic and he told me that they were doing scientific studies at the polar ice caps.

"We found evidence of an extra terrestrial gas leaking into the atmosphere we think it arrived in parts of a large meteorite that hit the earth during the Jurassic era. We started to study the effects of the gaseous substance. After a lengthy study we deduced that the gas could become harmful if there was enough of it in the atmosphere but we couldn't tell how long the gas had been leaking into the atmosphere.

"Studies showed that the gas was harmless but the scientists that conducted the tests didn't take into account the length of time that the gas was being poured into the atmosphere mixing with the pollution in the air and how it would mutate.

"The mixture did something no one expected, it bonded with dead cells, Human cells to be exact. The recently deceased woke up and just had the most basic brain functions, the most basic need the need to eat so.

"They turned on the only food source available, us, then something happened when the gas bonded with the dead, it became a virus transmitted through the zombies' saliva. One bite would infect a living person and within a few hours to a few days depending on how bad the injury was, the person would become one of them."

I asked him whether, over time, the dead would die eventually with there being no more food about for them. He didn't know but he said that the zombies in his opinion didn't need to eat but it would still take a long time for the zombies to die, that's if the virus didn't mutate further. If that happens it would be a disaster.

The day came when I was ready to return for my family. Doctor Morgan made sure that I had everything I needed; guns, ammo, vehicles, food and even a radio scanner. All I had to do was bide my time.

I took a boat from the rig to the mainland, then a reinforced car to the town where the compound was. It had been over four months since Jerry tried to have me killed and I hoped that my wife and kids were still alright.

The only problems I had were how was I going to get into the compound and would Elaine believe it was me as my face had changed so much.

I couldn't think about that at the moment, I had to concentrate on how to get into the compound. I parked on a hill overlooking the compound, there were two men guarding on top of the gates but the place was crawling with zombies.

Later that night I found an abandoned farmhouse. The house was completely empty and there was no electricity but I blocked myself in for the night and got something to eat.

I turned on the radio scanner and fell asleep. About four o'clock in the morning, I was awoken by the sound of a voice. It sounded like that piece of shit, Carl.

I listened for a while. They were in need of fuel and asking for assistance. I realised that was my way in, all I needed was a fuel truck. I contacted them.

Connor: "Hello there, can you hear me, hello."

Carl: "Hello, I'm Carl, can you help us we need fuel."

Connor: "Hello Carl, I'm Bill. Yes you're in luck my friend I have a tanker full but it'll cost you."

Carl: "Ok what do you want?" he asked with worry in his voice.

Connor: "Don't panic Carl, all I want in return is two or three weeks' room and board and I will give you as much fuel as you can handle."

Carl: "Yes, no problem, that's great. We can do that, when will you get here?"

Connor: "Give me your location."

Carl gave me the location and I told him that it would take me at least three days to get there.

Connor: "Would you be able to hold out till then?"

Carl: "Yes we should be fine. Tell me something Bill, do I know you?"

I thought to myself, that's it I've been rumbled. Carl had recognised my voice. I stayed calm and answered him.

Connor: "I don't know, maybe, but I doubt it why."

Carl: "I thought I recognised your voice, it doesn't matter we'll see you in three days, and thanks Bill."

Connor: "No problem, I'll contact you when I'm close, over and out."

I drove around for two days looking for a fuel tanker. Just when I was about to give up I spotted one in behind a garage but the area was full of zombies. How was I going to get to it?

I was running out of time so I pulled up outside the garage and started to rev the engine. That attracted the zombies and they started to gather around the car. I drove off slowly up the road they followed me.

When I got to a clear spot I got out of the car. I grabbed a couple of guns and started firing. I cut most of them down, got back into the car and drove back to the garage.

When I got there I could see that some of the zombies were still hanging around. There was only a few of them, hopefully I would be able to handle them.

I got out of the car with my guns and headed over to the tanker. When I got there I got in to the tanker and looked at the gauge, the tanker was full thanks be to god and the keys were in it. The luck was with me, I hoped it would hold out till this was over.

I went back to the car and got the radio scanner then run back to the tanker firing at the zombies being careful not to hit the tanker full of fuel. I got in and drove away, stopping on the road about a mile from the compound and got on to the radio. Jerry answered.

Jerry: "Where are you?"

Connor: "I'm about a mile out coming in from the east to where you are. I'm coming hot and heavy so be ready."

I didn't trust Jerry or his cohorts, so I decided to booby-trap the tanker just in case. I strapped the remote to my wrist to make it look like I and the booby-trap were linked.

I drove to the compound and they opened the first set of gates. I was told to drive in slowly and when I did the gates locked behind me. Then I heard shots.

I looked up I saw Mat and Brian with sniper rifles taking out the zombies that had got in and when they were all dead the second set of gates opened up. I was told to drive into the middle of the compound.

When I stopped the tanker I was told to stay inside the cab until I got further orders. There was something wrong, I looked into the wing mirror and saw armed men surrounding the tanker.

Peter: "Get out slowly with your hands above your head."

Connor: "What's this all about?"

Peter: "We decided why have a little when we can have the lot," he said smugly.

Connor: "Calm down friend, I'm not armed I'm going to put my hands down I want to show you something."

I put my hands down slowly and rolled up my sleeve.

Peter: "What's that thing on your arm?"

Connor: "It's insurance, the tanker's wired up. If you shoot me the explosives go off, if you try to remove this from my wrist they go off, if you try to disarm the explosives they go off. The resulting explosion will take out this whole compound and most of the people in it."

Peter: "Wait here a minute," he said nervously.

Peter ran to the living quarters and a few minutes later he returned.

Peter: "Mat get your ass down here. Go and look at the bomb underneath that thing and see if it can be disarmed.

Mat: "There's nothing I can do, it's a professional job."

Peter: "Ok go around and fill the tank, then store your stuff in there and go and see the doctor. We'll stick to the deal and after you do that the boss wants to meet you.

I did as I was told after I stored my gear and went to see the doctor. To my surprise it was Elaine, I had forgotten that she acted as the doctor and I had to stop myself from wrapping my arms around her but I knew I couldn't let her know it was me just yet.

Over at the other side of the room sat Dominic, Sara and Louise. I was so glad that they were alright. Elaine turned to me and looked at me weirdly.

Connor: "Is there something wrong miss?"

Elaine: "Sorry for staring but for a minute there you looked like someone I lost, sorry, anyway what can I do for you?"

Connor: "I was told to come here."

Elaine: "It's only to get checked to make sure you're not infected."

After Elaine examined me I headed back to the compound there I met Mat and Brian.

Mat: "Who are you?"

Connor: "I'm Bill, why? Who do you think I am?"

Mat: "You're no explosive expert that's for sure so tell us who you are and what you want. It's no coincidence that you just happened to be around just when we needed fuel. We aren't that lucky so tell us who you are."

I was going to have to trust someone I knew I was going to need help pulling this thing off so I decided to confide in Brian and Mat.

Conner: "It's me, Connor."

Brian: "Bullshit. Connor's dead and you don't even look like Connor."

Connor: "Peter shot me in the face, I was lucky other scavengers found me and saved my life. They're based on an oil rig off the coast. I'm here to get my family and whoever else wants to come with me."

Mat: "If Peter did shoot you why did he do it?"

Connor: "Jerry told him to, he wanted to take over. I take it that's what happened?"

Brian: "Yes he took over with the help of John, Carl and Peter. It took place before we knew what had happened. They put me and Mat and some of the others in a makeshift cell for about a month and threatened to kick us out if we didn't join them. We thought they were bluffing until they took one of the people out and made him stand between the two gates. They closed the inner gates and opened the outer gates and we could hear the horrible screams. After that we had no other choice but to join them.

Mat: "I'm still not fully convinced that you're telling the truth."

Connor: "Ok do you remember when we first got here we went to have a look at the armoury. You were like a kid in a sweet shop and then you showed Brian and me how to use the shot guns. How would I know that, and Brian you're the one that put my name forward to be the leader."

Brian: "Shit it is you, Connor," he said with excitement on his face.

Connor: "Calm down, we don't need anybody's suspicions raised. Now are you two with me when I make my move?"

Mat: "Yes, just give us the nod."

Connor: "I'll speak to you boys later. I'll tell you the plan then but we shouldn't be seen together too much."

I went to meet with the boss just as I was told to do. Jerry liked to be called the boss, what a dick head.

Jerry: "I'm Jerry, just call me boss."

Connor: "I'm Bill, just call me Bill. You know your men didn't have to hold me by gun point. I'll make you a deal, I'll call here every three months and fill your fuel tank for two weeks of R and R."

Jerry: "It's a deal, you're a pleasure to do business with."

For two days I had been gathering all the detail I could. I spoke to Mat and Brian.

Connor: "Did you find out who will go and who won't. Who's with us and who's with Jerry?"

Brian: "We can't do that. We don't know who to trust. Jerry keeps us away from the main population."

Mat: "We do know that there are fifteen men that are close to Jerry, most of them stay around him on the top floor. Jerry took it over after you were gone. There are about six men on patrol at night."

Connor: "Here's the plan. You two take care of the men that are patrolling, try not to kill them if you don't have to. I'll go get the weapons, and after you have finished with the men wait for me outside the living quarters.

Brian: "Did you tell Elaine yet?"

Connor: "No, I'll do that after I secure the guns. Let's get to it, there's no time to waste."

When I had sorted out the weapons I went to talk to Elaine. When I got to where she was sleeping I put my hand over her mouth and dragged her to the next room. I told her who I really was.

At the start she didn't believe me, then I told her some personal things about our lives together, things that no one else could know. She started to cry and hugged me. I told her the plan and told her to get the kids ready and that we were leaving.

Elaine: "What do you mean leaving? Where are we going to go? There is nowhere else to go."

Connor: "Yes there is, an oil rig off the coast. There is a small self-sufficient community. They saved my life and told me that I was welcome to come back and I could bring as many people as I could. Now, please Elaine go do as I tell you. We'll be leaving sometime after daybreak."

Brian and Mat took care of the men that were patrolling then the three of us started to disarm everyone as quietly as we could. At daybreak we woke Jerry and his men and we marched them downstairs and into the compound. By this time all the people were gathered in the compound and I explained what Jerry and the others had done to me and why.

Connor: "I have found a place that is safe, the people there have told me that you are all welcome. I'm not going to force any of you to come with me. It's your choice, but make it quick, remember it's either come with me or stay with Jerry. Whoever is coming you've got ten minutes to decide. Mat go and get the trucks ready."

When time came to go everyone, except Jerry and people loyal to him, declined. When they realised they would be alone they changed their minds.

Jerry: "Now look Connor, we've had our differences but we can put that all behind us, we could let bygones be bygones and anyway it was Peter that shot you not me."

Connor: "Ok Jerry."

Mat: "Wait a minute here. That piece of shit, his men and his little spies treated us all like their own personal play things. Not counting what they did to some of the women."

Jerry: "There is no evidence that we did anything wrong."

Connor: "He's right."

Brian: "You're going to take his word over ours."

Connor: "There's one way to settle this a show of hands. Do we let Jerry and his people come with us or do we leave them here."

I looked around two people voted to bring them with us.

Connor: "There, you have your answer Jerry. Now have one of your men open the gates before we drive through them."

Jerry: "Yu won't get away with this, we will hunt you all down and feed you to the zombies bit by bit."

As we left the compound I could hear Jerry shouting abuse and threatening that he would kill us all. Then Elaine noticed.

Elaine: "Connor we're in trouble. Carl is getting a rocket launcher ready," she roared.

Connor: "Don't panic sweetheart, I have it all under control."

I took the remote control for the explosives under the fuel tanker then I pressed the button. A few seconds later the compound exploded. You brought this on yourself Jerry, I thought to myself.

Elaine put her arm around me as I was driving and I thought to myself I haven't been this happy in years. I hoped and prayed that I had done the right thing by taking the survivors with me.

The journey took two weeks to get to the coast because there were more of those zombies than there had been before so we had to avoid highly populated areas and a lot of roads were blocked by burned out cars and abandoned vehicles of all descriptions. This meant we had to take large detours.

When we eventually arrived at the docks it was barricaded and closed off. The large fence in front of us opened up and I spotted what looked like at least fifteen to twenty well-armed men. I was about turn back when one of them beckoned us to enter.

Brian: "What do we do now Connor?"

Connor: "The only thing we can do, we drive in slowly."

Elaine: "Are you sure we can trust these people?"

Connor: "I'm not sure of anyone or anything anymore but we have no other choice at the moment. Brian radio the other trucks and tell them to follow us and tell them to be ready for anything."

We drove in and when the trucks stopped I got out and walked over to one of the armed men.

He asked if we were infected and I replied, "No." He asked who I was I told him my name. He laughed and introduced himself as Sergeant Jay Laverty. "Just call me Jay," he said.

Connor: "What's so funny Jay?"

Jay: "You'll have to forgive me, but when Doctor Morgan told me about you I thought it was futile waiting here for your arrival. I would have bet you'd be dead by now."

Connor: "I didn't see you or you're men here are on the oil rig when I was last here."

Jay: "You wouldn't have, we arrived a few days after your departure. We struck a deal with Morgan and the others if they would let us live on the rig, we would in exchange give them our expertise."

Connor: "What expertise do you have?"

Jay: "We do supply runs, well all the dangerous stuff to be honest. We're army, we're trained for dangerous missions, admittedly we were never prepared for this kind of thing. Anyway they tell us where to find the items they need, and we go and get them. We've being doing this since we got here."

Connor: "What's your take on the doctor and the other's?"

Jay: "A little strange I guess. Living on an oil rig for a few years with virtually no contact with the outside world would make anybody act strangely. But they seem harmless."

Connor: "So what do my people and I do now?"

Jay: "Get your people to disembark the vehicles and bring whatever supplies you have with you and get onto the boats provided. How many came with you Connor?"

Connor: "About seventy. Will there be enough room for everybody because if there isn't we're going, I'm not leaving any of them behind."

Jay: "Don't worry we have room for all of your people. Now let's get started, I don't want to be here any longer than we have to be."

It took around half an hour to get to the oil rig and we went up the ladder one by one to the main platform above us. I was the last one up other than some of the soldiers.

When I got to the platform my people were surrounded by armed soldiers. Doctor Morgan was there to.

Connor: "What the hell's going on doctor? You said to bring as many people with me that would come and when I do we're all treated like we're criminals."

Morgan: "You have to understand Connor, I can't risk the infection getting out here so you and your people will have to go into quarantine."

Connor: "For how long?"

Morgan: "Seven days. It's the only way to make sure. The doctors will check you all over one by one and when you clear your examination you'll be given quarters of your own."

Connor: "Ok doctor, we understand."

We were led into a part of the rig that didn't seem to be used often and over the next seven days one by one we were examined extensively. When the quarantine period was over Doctor Morgan assigned all of us living quarters and work.

Elaine was put to work in the hospital. Mat, Brian and I were put in charge of security on our part of the rig and everything was going great until one of our people went missing.

She was nowhere to be found and the consensus was that she couldn't take any more and had committed suicide. There was nothing strange about this, unfortunately, these things happen.

As the months went by people started to notice strange things like some of our own falling sick and then disappearing without a trace. This had happened to ten people so far, six of ours and four of Jay's men.

But none of Morgan's people seemed to be falling ill, in fact since we got here Morgan and his people seemed to be – I don't know – healthier than when I first met them. Maybe I was imagining it. I decided to approach Doctor Morgan and I went to his office. I knocked on the door.

Morgan: "Come in," he said loudly.

Connor: "Could I speak to you Doctor, if you're not busy."

Morgan: "Of course Connor, I'm never too busy to have a chat with you, now sit down and tell me what's on your mind."

Connor: "Six of the group that came with me and four of Jay's soldiers have gone missing over the past couple of months and that's not counting the woman that went missing just after we arrived."

Morgan: "Ha, I was hoping to talk to you about this, the girl that supposedly killed herself, didn't."

Connor: "Why tell me this now and not when she went missing and where is she?"

Morgan: "Look Connor, a small team of my people noticed irregularities in this lady Joann's blood work and found that the virus maybe mutating. She came to me because she was feeling, as she put it, odd, so I thought it was better to quarantine her. I waited for you to come to me. If I had gone to you someone could have picked up that there might be something wrong."

Connor: "None of my people would have picked up on anything. All you needed to do was send for me, no one would've known any different."

Morgan: "I wasn't worried about your people, it's mine. If the general population had any idea that your people had brought a new form of the virus onto the rig there would be pandemonium."

Connor: "I understand, so what new virus did we bring with us?"

Morgan: "It's not so much new, it seems to be a mutation of the old one."

Connor: "So we have to go back into quarantine I'll tell them."

Morgan: "No it's too late for that. A couple of my people have died. I've managed to keep it between a few doctors and myself. So if we keep this between us for now Connor only you me and a couple of doctors know, so keep it quiet until we know more."

I left Doctor Morgan's office with a feeling of imminent doom. I didn't fully believe his explanation, he was too calm to be telling the truth. I waited till that night when Elaine got back to our quarters.

Elaine: "Hello love, what's wrong with you? Are you alright Connor?" she inquired with a worried tone.

Connor: "I don't think I am. I'm starting to think coming here was a mistake a big mistake."

She looked at me with a bewildered expression on her face. "But why," she asked.

Connor: "Because there's something going on here. There have been a few disappearances that I can't explain."

Elaine: "Have you spoke to Doctor Morgan about this?"

Connor: "Yes, I spoke to Morgan early today, but I don't believe what he told me."

Then I went on to tell Elaine about what Morgan had said and that I had doubts about the whole situation. To my surprise Elaine didn't disagree with me.

Elaine: "I didn't want to say anything but there have been a few things that don't add up about Doctor Morgan and his people."

Connor: "Like what?"

Elaine: "They never seem to get sick, we never see them eat and they never seem to be agitated or irritated. The only time I have seen one of them anywhere near the hospital was because there was something wrong was that man, Doctor Eldridge his hand was badly burned so he was brought into the hospital and then before I could take a proper good look at the wound, two others came in and whisked him away."

Connor: "That doesn't mean anything. What's wrong with that?"

Elaine: "I took a quick glimpse of the burn as they were escorting Eldridge out of the hospital. It was a first-degree burn. By rights he should have been screaming in pain even with strong painkillers. And the people that had this mutation of the virus, I did some of the blood work there was no evidence of any virus at all in any of the blood samples. And none of them passed through the hospital. If they were sick I would have been there to treat them, also they would have come to me quicker than Doctor Morgan."

Connor: "Tell me something Elaine, what age would you say Morgan was."

Elaine: "I know his age, he's around seventy-three."

Connor: "How do you know that?"

Elaine: "Because he was a well-known doctor until ten years ago, when Morgan and twenty scientists went on an expedition to the farthest most point of the South Pole. After he and the other scientists got back they seemed to drop off the radar. There were rumours that they had made several trips back to the south pole since then with different scientists but each time they also went into reclusion after that."

Connor: "What are the odds that every person here, apart from us of course was part of these expeditions?"

Elaine: "But what has his age got to do with all of this?"

Connor: "Maybe nothing, but he looks very spry for an over seventy-year-old man and come to think of it so do the others and they all seem a lot more vigorous since we got here."

The next night I got Mat, Brian and Jay together. When we met I told them my suspicions. They thought that I was being paranoid but then I told them what Elaine had told me.

Jay: "I think Conner's right, I don't know about the rest of you, something's wrong here. Four of my men are missing, if they had been sick I'd have known about it. One day they were there, the next day they weren't. That's not sick, that's disappeared."

Mat: "Let's face it, we've all got the Wiggins about this place."

Brian: "So what do we do about it?"

Connor: "We investigate. We look for anything out of the ordinary and gather information. We'll meet back here in one week when we'll find out if we're in trouble or not."

Brian: "Why do we have to wait for a week?"

Connor: "Look, we'll meet as usual like we do all the time, have a laugh and joke but don't talk about this not to anyone or each other until next week. If Morgan suspects I didn't believe him, at the very least he'll have me watched he knows who I would confide in so he may have you watched too so be careful."

For a week I tried to get evidence to prove my theories but to no avail, maybe I was being paranoid. I decided to call it all off because I was convinced that I was making something out of nothing.

When I got to the meeting place, Jay, Brian and Mat were waiting for me. I told them that maybe I was wrong and that I couldn't find a thing to prove my allegations. Mat and Jay said maybe I was mistaken because they couldn't find anything either. Just as we were about to go back to our quarters, Brian said, "Does no one want to hear what I found?"

Connor: "What did you find?"

Brian: "I think I found a secret lab. The glass was toughened and frosted but I'm sure there's something in there."

Jay: "How do you know it was a secret lab?" he asked sarcastically.

Brian: "I'm an architect and electrician by trade, there's a corridor below Morgan's office that shouldn't be there. It didn't feel right since I first went into that area but it didn't dawn on me till a few days ago. I went to have another look when I noticed electrical wires running through the walls of the corridor. That wasn't right, there's not meant to be anything there that needs power."

Mat: "Maybe it was for the lights, maybe they wanted to hide some extended wiring."

Brian: "Look up."

Mat: "Ok what am I looking at?"

Brian: "Do you see the wires?"

Mat: "No, there aren't any wires there."

Brian: "Precisely my point the wires are covered everywhere and they have wire mesh underneath in case the wire drops. When I looked there was none of that so I groped around for about ten minutes and found a hidden release.

"A door opened up, I went in and hid in the shadows until the coast was clear. There were men in white lab coats going in through automatic glass doors. I tried to get in but we need a key card. I can't do it on my own I thought maybe Mat could bypass the lock. I don't know what's in there but it looks like something they want to keep to themselves."

We made a plan to go in the next night and see what these people were at.

At twelve o'clock the following night we met up in the corridor beneath Doctor Morgan's office. Brian opened the hidden door and we quietly went through. We came to a frosted glass door which was unlocked and we walked in. On each side of the corridor there was a glass wall, no doors, but just a wall and a metal floor.

Jay: "That was easy."

Brian: "Yep too easy."

Connor: "I don't like this, there's something wrong. Jay you go back the way we came and keep an eye out. If there's trouble warn us."

Jay: "No problem."

When Jay went back, we went on, halfway down the glass corridor a steel wall came shooting down behind us, then a few seconds later another steel door came shooting down in front of us we were trapped.

Brian: "I knew it, I said it was too easy someone must have told them we were coming here."

Mat: "No one could have told, no one knew we were coming here."

Brian: "What about Jay? He's not here."

Connor: "He's not here because I sent him back, remember."

A few seconds later a voice sounded over the intercom. It sounded like Doctor Morgan.

Morgan: "I'm sorry for keeping you chaps. Tell me do you know what happened to the curious cat? No, well you're going to find out very soon."

Then we heard a sound like someone had turned on a faulty switch only louder. I felt a sudden electrical shock and then blackness.

When I opened my eyes, Mat, Brian and I were strapped to a table. When we were fully awake the tables were turned upright. There was

Morgan looking at me with a smile of victory on his face.

Mat: "It was Jay, he informed on us. You were right Brian."

Brian: "Well not entirely, look over there."

We could see two of Morgan's men dragging a beaten and knocked out Jay.

Connor: "Then who warned you that we were coming?"

Then we heard Brian laughing, Mat asked him what he was laughing at.

Connor: "It was him Mat, he informed on us."

Mat: "Brian you are a son of a bitch, a dirty traitor, I hope you rot in hell."

Then Brian took his hands out of the straps and stood beside Morgan. Then the two men strapped Jay into the table.

Connor: "What do you gain from betraying us Brian?"

Brian: "Doctor Morgan said that I would be given the highest reward possible if I helped him. It's a dog eat dog world out there, literally. I'm sorry but I've got a chance to be somebody, for once I had to take it."

Morgan: "Oh that reminds me, as for your payment Brian take him to the processing room."

Brian: "No way, you said you would give me the highest reward," he roared.

Morgan: "But you are getting the highest reward possible. Being part of us is the highest rewards. Now take him away."

I could hear Brian scream in fear as they dragged him away, I could tell he knew what they were going to do to him.

Connor: "This processing room, what happens there?"

Morgan: "You see Connor, it's people like you that keep me and the others alive. To put it bluntly we inject you. We discovered a process that takes a body and breaks it down into a serum. We inject it and this way we can stay alive for ever and you brought enough raw materials to keep us alive for a long, long time."

Mat: "Are you crazy? You can't live forever by injecting melted human, you idiot."

Connor: "There's something else, the gas, there was something in the gas, something that changed you and then over a ten year period you exposed other scientists."

Morgan: "Smart man, your wife recognised me didn't she? I knew by the way she looked at me. With her being a nurse she would have read some of my medical papers."

Connor: "It's only a guess, but you and your friends had something to do with what went on in the last six months. All those deaths, for what?"

Morgan: "That was unexpected, the virus was just supposed to kill a certain group, a person with a type of abnormality, one that we had never seen before. Only twenty percent of the world's population has it. We couldn't detect the abnormality in a living specimen. The virus mutated when it killed these people. They came back to life and they passed on the virus. It was a miscalculation on our part."

Mat: "Why kill anybody?"

Morgan: "The twenty percent that had the abnormality would kill us. Our bodies couldn't take that serum it was like poison to us and the only way to find out who they were was blood taken from a dead body and we need live specimens to – shall we say – feed."

Connor: "You people are selfish, you turn the world to shit because you're afraid of death."

Morgan: "There's nothing selfish about keeping the greatest minds of this century alive for ever. Just think of what it would mean for the world, think of the leaps as the human race we could take."

Mat: "Yep, having you pricks live forever really has done wonders for humanity you dick," he said in an angry but sarcastic tone.

Morgan just looked at us and walked away. When Jay woke up we filled him in on what had been going on. A few minutes later Morgan came back with three syringes' and injected us with whatever was in them. It must have been potent stuff I think I passed out almost straight away.

I was awoken by Elaine, she was slapping my face. I could hear her telling me to wake up and when I told her that I was already awake she started to untie me from the table.

Connor: "What are you doing here? How did you find us?"

Elaine: "Over the last week I followed you and I've been talking to the people. Some believe that there's something going on, some don't and the rest want to live in ignorance. We have to do something now. I overheard a couple of them talking they said something about a serum and they'll be processing the rest within a few weeks and they don't suspect a thing. I don't know what that means but I don't like the sound of it. I think we should take as many people with us as we can then go and get our tails out of here."

I remembered Brian and ran to the processing room. Brian was in a glass tube, it looked like he was being melted. Slowly he opened his eyes, "Help me," he pleaded. Then I could see a tear rolling down his face and then he closed his eyes.

Mat put his hand on my shoulder.

Mat: "He's done, we can't do anything for him now let's go."

Elaine got the kid's and whoever else was coming with us as we all headed to where the boats were kept they were gone.

Mat: "Crap, what are we going to do now?"

I looked behind us and Morgan was standing there with his men.

Morgan: "Did you think I would let you go so easily? We need you to live."

Connor: "So this is the fate of every person here."

Morgan: "Not every person, the women will breed with us and we will rebuild the human race in our image. We will be gods."

Mat: "You're mad, you're all mad."

Connor: "Why did you change some women into yourself?"

Morgan: "Do you not think we tried? The process kills the female form so give up, at least you'll know that your women will live on."

Connor "What about that woman Joann, how did she die?"

Morgan: "She was a test subject, unfortunate, but these things happen."

Just then Jay took his hand gun from his holster, he aimed it at Doctor Morgan and pulled the trigger. Jay shot him right between the eyes. Morgan fell backwards and landed with a crash.

Jay: "I'll do the same to each and every one of you until you get the boats and bring them to us."

Suddenly Morgan stood up and laughed. He put his fingers into the hole in his forehead and pulled the bullet out.

Morgan: "It'll take more than that to kill us. You see the gas gives us the ability to regenerate any wound."

Suddenly with pain in his voice and a vest full of C4 explosives wired up to a remote detonator attached to him Brian stepped from the shadows. He was disfigured and the skin was dropping from his body like wax drops from a lit candle.

Brian: "Where's the boats Morgan?"

Morgan: "Now Brian, you know you won't push that button."

Brian: "Look at me ,you moron, now do you think I won't push it."

Morgan: "What with all your friends here? I don't think so."

Brian: "I think they would rather go quickly and not like this. You better hurry Morgan, I don't know how long I can hold onto this detonator. Everybody if you stay you'll end up like this sooner are later go and be safe."

Morgan: "Get them the boats now. Connor you're just delaying the inevitable."

Morgan's men brought the boats. Mat, Jay and I got all of our people in. Louise, Sara and Dominic hugged me then Elaine got them and herself into the boat.

Brian: "Go lads, be safe and I'm sorry."

Mat: "it's ok, Brian," he said with a smile.

Brian: "I said GO!" he roared.

Mat, Jay and I got in to the boats and started up the engines. As we were speeding away I could hear Morgan scream after us that this wasn't over and they would find us.

Then I heard a noise like a clash of thunder, I looked around at the oil rig and I could see a ball of fire. Brian had set off a chain reaction after the initial explosion several small ones exploded and the rig started to fall into the sea.

I hoped that was the last we would see of Morgan and his people. Unfortunately with what we had seen I wasn't too sure, but for now we were just glad to be alive and now we must seek safety soon or we would all die.

THE END

SUB-HUMAN EVOLUTION

2110 February14. Deep space rescue ship Orion.
Officer in charge: Captain Len Markus.
Destination: Capricorn 2.
Mission: classified.
Estimated time of arrival: 7 hours 43 minutes.

In the cold darkness of space the rescue vessel Orion has almost reached the end of her journey.

The Orion and her crew has been ordered to the outer rim of our galaxy to a new settlement on a small world called Capricorn 2. It has been the farthest that the human race has travelled.

Captain Markus and his crew were given orders to assist the vessel SS. Edmond that has been orbiting Capricorn 2 for the last four years.

As the Orion starts to approach its destination the crew starts to awaken from a three months cryogenic sleep.

As Captain Markus opens his eyes he sees Doctor Malone hovering over him.

Malone: "Take it easy captain, you'll feel weak for a while so when you're ready get up slowly."

Captain Markus nodded and started to cough. He slowly sat up and slid off the end of the bed and onto the floor. He put his hand on his forehead.

Markus: "Oh my god what's happening?" he said as he slouched to the floor.

Malone hurriedly rushed over to where the captain had fallen and helped him back onto the bed.

Malone: "Are you alright captain? I did tell you to take it slowly."

Markus: "Yep, I'm fine Doc, I just felt a little dizzy."

Malone: "You'll be fine captain, just take it easy for a few minutes it's a normal side effect from the cryogenic sleep"

Markus: "I know Doc, I've done this before."

Malone: "Yes I know sir, but nonetheless be careful, I want you to rest for a few minutes now take this," he said as he handed a small pill to the captain.

Markus: "What's this for?"

Malone: "It's for your stomach."

Markus: "It's alright there's nothing wrong with my stomach."

Malone: "I would advise you to take it captain."

Markus: "What did I say? I don't need it."

Malone: "Suit yourself." As Doctor Malone walked away from the captain he could hear Markus being sick. He turned back and stood beside the bed until the captain had finished. Markus wiped his mouth with the sleeve of his hospital gown and Malone handed him the little white pill and a glass of water.

Markus: "What the hell just happened? My god, that was embarrassing, I haven't done that since my days at training school."

Malone: "Take that pill, it'll make you feel better it'll just take a few minutes to work."

Markus: "So what's wrong, what happened to me?"

Malone: "There's nothing wrong with you. We've been in cryogenic sleep for over three months. It's a long time to be in an artificial sleep. What you have to remember is not many people have been out this far. The longer we stay asleep using this process the longer our bodies take to recover."

Markus: "Tell me Doc, where is the usual ship's Doctor."

Malone: "I don't know. The day before the ship departed I got my orders."

Just then Sergeant Lennon approached captain Markus. He stood at attention and saluted.

Lennon: "Sir, the crew is awake. What are your orders captain?"

Markus: "Who are these people sergeant?"

Lennon: "I haven't got a clue sir, there seems to have been a big shake up."

Markus: "Ok, make sure everybody gets something to eat then they can report to their posts. Tell the executive officers to meet me in the conference room and that includes you sergeant."

Lennon: "Very good sir," he said as he saluted, then sergeant Lennon turned and marched out.

Malone: "He's a little urgent isn't he? These military lifers make me nervous, I don't trust them."

Markus: "Have a little respect Doctor, Lennon is a soldier and a good one at that, he has saved my life a number of times, so watch what you say."

Malone: "Yes captain, I understand. I apologise for speaking out of turn."

Markus: "Don't look so glum Doc, I'm not a tyrant, you'll find I like things – to coin an old phrase – shipshape and Bristol fashion. If you respect that then we'll get on ok."

Malone: "Yes sir." As he was walking away the captain called to him, he looked around.

Markus: "Oh by the way Doctor, I want you at the briefing too, 1800 hours don't be late."

Malone: "Why me? I'm just a doctor."

Markus: "You're one of my executive officers I like to hear input from all my officers. You never know, you may see something that the rest of us might miss, stranger things have happened."

Malone: "I'll be there Captain, thank you."

Captain Markus got dressed and headed towards the briefing room. When he entered he saw his personal steward laying his meal on the table.

Markus: "Who are you?" he asked.

The steward answered, "Hennessey, sir."

Markus looked intensely at Hennessey.

Hennessey: "Sorry sir, did I do anything wrong?" he asked worriedly.

Markus: "No, you did nothing wrong, it's just that I'm not used to seeing so many new faces aboard my ship. You can go now Hennessey send Lt Gingili to me when he's finished his meal."

Hennessey: "Yes sir, I'll tell the Lt straight away, sir."

When Hennessey left the briefing room Captain Markus logged on to his computer console. He was surprised that he hadn't the clearance to find out what their mission was.

About a half an hour later, Lt Gingili entered. He stood to attention and saluted, "You wanted to see me sir?" he asked.

Captain Markus looked up from his computer screen.

Markus: "For god sake man, stand at ease and take a seat."

Gingili: "Yes sir, thank you sir."

Markus: "Let me ask you something Lt, how long have we served together?"

Gingili: "Almost seven years sir, why do you ask?"

Markus: "In all the years we've served together, have you ever seen a crew shake up like this before?"

Gingili: "My understanding is that this mission was put together in a rush."

Markus: "We've had rush jobs before but they've never changed almost all of the crew before. I haven't even got a high enough clearance to find out what we're doing here. I don't have a good feeling about this one. They've never kept me out of the loop before."

Gingili: "But you're the Captain, if anyone should be told what we're doing here it's you. If you don't mind me asking sir, what did they tell you?"

Markus: "They informed me that there would be a couple of personnel changes but this is ridiculous. Did you take a look at the personnel roster?"

Gingili: "I would have checked the roster straight away sir but as soon as I got on board they put me in the freezer."

Markus: "It was the same with me. There's something wrong here, I don't like it, I don't like it one bit. Have you looked at the rota yet?"

Gingili: "No sir, I haven't had a chance yet."

Captain Markus turned his screen around. "Have a look and tell me what you think."

Gingili: "Can I speak freely Captain?"

Markus: "Please do Lt Gingili."

Gingili: "There's something going on here sir I suspect the brass maybe doing something that they shouldn't that's why most of our men are gone. Look at this there are only seven of our original marines left. Sergeant Lennon, corporal Roberts, corporal Holland, privates Ramos McCourt and Carol and myself."

Markus: "And we only have under half a complement on board. 39 out of 83 members of the crew the bridge is full of new officers but why did they replace Williams for Hennessy?"

Gingili: "I can explain that Captain Williams' mother passed away the day before we got our orders."

Markus: "Ah, when we get back remind me to send my condolences to Williams. Who are these two? Professor Hughes and his assistant Doctor Fox?"

Gingili: "I know nothing about them Captain since we came out of deep sleep they've kept themselves to themselves. Captain this whole situation is ridiculous, sir."

Markus: "I know, but I have to follow orders just like everyone else."

Gingili: "So who's telling us what's what?"

Markus: "According to the computer Professor Hughes and Doctor Fox. Go back to your post I'll see if I can wrangle some more information from the good Professor."

Captain Markus made his way to the Professor's quarters and knocked on the door. A few seconds later the door opened.

Markus: "Professor Hughes?" he inquired.

Hughes: "That's me and what can I do for you?"

Markus: "I'm here to introduce myself, I'm Captain Markus."

Hughes: "Ha Captain," he said excitedly. "I've been looking forward to meeting you. Where are my manners? Come in Captain. To what do I owe the pleasure?"

Markus: "I would like to know more about this mission."

Hughes: "I can't do that, I'm sorry, well not just yet, all will be revealed when we get to Capricorn 2."

Markus: "Professor, I'm the Captain of this vessel and I demand to know what we're doing here."

Hughes: "With all due respect Captain I'm in charge of this mission not you you'll take your orders from me for the duration of this mission. All you have to do is take care of the ship and try not to crash into anything. So if that's all Captain, I have a lot work to do."

Markus: "Fine Professor, I'll alert you when we enter Capricorn space."

Hughes: "You do that and when we get there all will be revealed," he said as he showed Captain Markus out of his quarters, then he closed the door.

As Captain Markus headed to the bridge he heard someone call out to him. He turned around to see who it was. An officer stood in front of him and saluted.

Officer: "Sir an emergency communication," he said as he handed Markus a sheet of paper. He read the communication. It was an automated distress signal from Capricorn 2.

Markus: "That's all, I'll take care of this."

Captain Markus returned to Professor Hughes quarters he knocked on the door and Professor Hughes answered.

Hughes: "What now Captain you do know that I have a lot of work to do?" he said with an annoyed tone.

Markus: "We intercepted a repeating automatic distress signal coming from Capricorn 2. I didn't know that there was a settlement on that planet, so what's going on?"

Hughes: "No one did. The settlement was classified and we must get there immediately. Captain get your men ready I'll be starting the briefing in a few minutes."

Later in the briefing room Captain Markus and the other officers waited for Professor Hughes the door opened the Professor entered the room and walked to the podium. Everybody went silent.

Hughes: "Two years ago we established a settlement on Capricorn 2. Three months later a structure was found it was built about several thousand years ago. This meant that we had definite proof of extraterrestrial life. It was then that the core had seen fit to classify the planet and put it out of bounds. It took a year and a half to dig down to find the opening."

Malone: "Why did it take so long to get into the structure?"

Hughes: "Whatever the outer walls were made of they couldn't break

149

through. They tried everything from diamond bit drills to laser drills, nothing worked so they had to dig till they found their way in."

Markus: "When they eventually made their way into the structure what was found?"

Hughes: "They found remains of two extraterrestrial corpses they were found deep in the centre of the structure almost perfectly preserved."

Roberts: "Just the two bodies? The reason I ask is if there was an indigenous population on this world wouldn't there have been more bodies or more structures?"

Hughes: "The scientists guessed the structure could have been some sort of temple. Maybe there was some sort of global cataclysmic destruction or a war they think that these two poor unfortunates came here for safety of course it's only a guess but who's to know what we might find in the future?"

Markus: "So what are we doing here?"

Hughes: "The remains and the artefacts that were recovered in the structure have to be transported back to earth. The intelligence that we could discover from these artefacts could be highly beneficial to mankind we must take all care to get these items to earth in one piece."

Markus: "So you're telling us we're delivery boys now."

Hughes: "No you're protection. If these artefacts get into the wrong hands it could be a disaster. The SS Edmond will be handling the removal of the items and we'll be handling the security. We'll be escorting the Edmond home. We don't expect any problems but it's better to be safe than sorry. But now things have changed with this distress call from the settlement on the planet we need to contact the Edmond, my assistant Doctor Fox is handling that."

Doctor Fox entered the briefing room and whispered to Professor Hughes.

Hughes: "Doctor Fox has informed me that there is no response from the SS Edmond, how long to Capricorn Two captain?"

Gingili: "Approximately fifteen minutes Professor."

As the Orion reached its destination they homed in view of the Edmond.

Gingili: "The power seems to be fluctuating. The ships dead Captain."

Markus: "Corporal Roberts take Ramos, Carroll and four of the new recruits and take a shuttle get a closer look at the Edmond."

Roberts: "Yes sir."

Corporal Roberts and his team got suited up and launched the shuttle. As they got closer to the SS Edmond they could see some superficial damage.

Markus: "Pan left Ramos, look at that there's been a hull breach."

Fox: "They were attacked, that would explain why we couldn't contact them."

Markus: "I don't think so. Ramos get as close to the breach as you can. They weren't attacked the breach happened from the inside."

Fox: "Then they were boarded by hostiles."

Markus: "I doubt it the Edmond is the Orion's brother ship there are only two ways she can be boarded, permission from the bridge or an override code and the only ones that have the code is headquarters."

Hughes: "And me, they give it to me in case of an emergency."

Roberts: "Sir, do you read me sir?"

Markus: "Yes what is it Roberts?"

Roberts: "What are our orders sir, do we board her or come back home?"

Markus: "Board her corporal and be careful, we don't know what happened yet we're sending you over the override code."

A few minutes later they docked the shuttle and boarded the Edmond.

Robert's: "Sir the gravity has been deactivated we'll make our way to the bridge and reactivate the power systems. That way we can close the blast doors and cut off the breach."

Markus: "Good idea do that."

When Roberts and his team entered the bridge, they were surprised to see that the place was ransacked.

Roberts: "Sir, the bridge has been ripped apart and there seems to be blood all over the place. I think whoever did this is long gone and the bridge crew long dead."

Corporal Ramos started getting the ship up and running.

Ramos: "What a mess someone did a real number on this thing."

Roberts: "Never mind the commentaries just get the power going this place is starting to give me the creeps."

Ramos: "Ok when I tell you press the red blue and green buttons in that order on the console above me. Say when you're ready sir."

Roberts: "Right I'm here, let me see red blue green alright ready."

Ramos: "Now."

As Corporal Roberts pressed the buttons on the console they could hear the generators struggling to start up then the power started to flicker wildly then everything went dark.

Roberts: "Oh good job Ramos," he said sarcastically.

Ramos: "Wait for it."

Suddenly the power went on and illuminated the bridge. There was blood and body parts everywhere.

Ramos: "Oh dear lord, it was a freaking massacre."

Markus: "What's happening there Roberts?"

Roberts: "Everybody on the bridge has been literally taken apart there are bits of them everywhere."

Ramos: "Captain, I've found the logs. The equipment here is to badly damaged to view them but I can send the data back to the Orion."

Markus: "Do that then take a look for any survivors and get back here."

Roberts: "Yes sir."

Markus: "It sounds like there was some sort of attack but there is something wrong with this whole scene, who would have the balls to attack a first-class battle-ready star ship."

Hughes: "Now we know what happened they were attacked, end of story. We'll have to take the cargo back to earth. We need to get to the settlement now. Captain get a shuttle ready."

Markus: "No professor, I can't do that."

Fox: "You'll do as you're told, remember the professor's in charge you do as he says."

Markus: Not any more, a military vessel has been attacked. Regulations state that all other commands are suspended, so till we find out what the hell is going on you do as I say."

Hughes: "Captain, I need to get to the scientific facility on the ground. We need to pick up the cargo and all the data now."

Markus: "We will professor, but only when we find out what attacked the SS Edmond. Besides we've tried to contact the settlement and we can't get any response. Odds are whatever happened on the Edmond also may have happened at the settlement so we'll take one step at a time."

Fox: "You will do as Professor Hughes requests or I will personally recommend you be court marshalled."

Markus: "Doctor Fox if you get in my way once more I will have you removed and put in the brig."

Gingili: "Sir, the SS Edmond's logs are ready to view."

Markus: "Put them up on the view screen Lt."

2110. Feb. 3. Captain Edwards' personal log SS Edmond.

The crew has just come out of deep sleep I've been in touch with the scientific team on the planet there seems to be some sort of disturbance down there they told me they had it under control and to wait till they contact me again but I think I'll send a squad down anyway to find out just what's going on.

2110. Feb. 3. Captain Edwards' personal logs SS Edmond.

Carver and his men couldn't get anywhere near the research facility, there's something badly wrong down there. There's some sort riot and they're killing each other. The facility staff has barricaded themselves inside and they won't answer communications. Now we've lost contact with Carver and his squad.

2110. Feb. 3. Captain Edwards' personal logs SS Edmond.

Thank god Lt Carver got back in contact after two hours of radio silence, he reports that the situation has become out of control. Carver has two men injured, luckily enough the injuries aren't life-threatening, just some deep gashes and bruises. A few stitches and a bit of rest and they'll be fine. I have ordered them home until we can gather more information about what's going on.

2110. Feb. 4. Captain Edwards personal logs SS Edmond.

We still can't get in touch with the research facility. We're going to try to infiltrate the facility again tomorrow and we're going to try to find a way in without being seen but I don't hold out much hope. According to the facilities blue prints once lock down is activated the place is locked down tighter than a drum.

2110. Feb. 4. Captain Edwards personal logs SS Edmond.

I've scrapped the idea of going back in for the moment. Besides, something strange has happened to one of the men that was injured at the facility. His skin has started to disintegrate, his body seems to be mutating. The doctors don't have a clue what's happening to him and none of them has ever seen anything like it. He has also become quite violent a few hours ago he attacked one of the medical staff and bit a lump of flesh out of the Doctor's arm. We've had to put him into a cryogenic sleep in the quarantine area near the docking port as far away from the crew as possible. I don't need them finding out about this just yet as I don't want to risk undue panic until we know what's causing this change.

2110. Feb. 5. Captain Edwards' personal logs SS Edmond.

I suspect that the scientific team on the planet have been dabbling in more than digging up old ruins I think they have been testing some sort of weapon, maybe biological. Two more of the men that were injured have been exhibiting the same symptoms within a twenty-four hour period. They don't look human anymore, they've become highly aggressive and they seem to be turning into another species. Within the last few hours the medical Doctor that was injured is now showing the same symptoms. At least they haven't lost their intelligence, that's one good thing, we can still communicate with them.

2110. Feb. 6. Captain Edwards' personal logs SS Edmond.
I wish I knew what was going on. The Doctors say that the three crew that we quarantined should be dead or at least in great pain but they aren't. They're starting to mutate even further. We're still trying to contact the scientists on Capricorn 2 to see if they know something that can help but still no luck.

Suddenly the screen started to fade out.

Markus: "Is that it is that all we have?"

Gingili: "the data was badly damaged sir, but there is one more entry on Feb 8th. It's a little distorted, probably due to the damage the bridge sustained."

Markus: "ok let's see it put it up on the screen."

2110. Feb. 8. Captain Edwards personal logs SS Edmond.
The three infected crewmen somehow escaped from quarantine and they attacked a number of the crew. The infection spread throughout the ship and I don't know what my men have turned into but whatever it is we can't kill them, nothing works, the whole crew are ether infected or dead. There are only two of us left now Lt Martin and myself. I suspect that the settlement is overrun as well. If this infection reaches earth no one will be able to stop it so Martin and I are going to stop this here. We're programming the ship for a collision course with the settlement. This log will be ejected and hopefully found by the Orion. May god have mercy on our souls.

Lt. Martin: "Sir they're getting in I can't stop them."

Edward's: "Come over here help me programme the computer."

As captain Markus and the crew in the briefing room looked on in horror they could see Captain Edwards and Lt Martin being savagely ripped apart then the screen went black.

A deathly silence fell over the briefing room.

Hughes: "What do we do now Captain Markus?"

Markus: "Roberts is heading to the briefing room, we'll find out what he found first and what the hell those things were.

A few minutes later L.T. Roberts entered the briefing room. His face looked like all the blood had been drained from him.

Roberts: "I'm here to make my report sir," he said, as he seemed to stare through them.

Markus: "What did you see over there soldier?"

Roberts: "As we were investigating the Edmond we came across some of the crew, they were mutilated beyond all recognition. We couldn't find any survivors."

Markus: "Is there any evidence of what might have done this?"

Roberts: "Yes sir, but I can't describe them, they were horrible, they weren't human, they were something else but they were also dead."

Fox: "Did you bring one back so we could study it?"

Markus: "We're not bringing one of those things on board."

Fox: "But its dead it can't do us any harm."

Markus: "I don't care, I'm not going to risk any sort infection on this ship."

Fox: "Professor, order him to do it."

Hughes: "No Doctor Fox, I'm with him on this besides he's in charge now."

Markus: "Ok Roberts, dismissed. Go and get something to eat and some rest."

Roberts: "Thank you sir, but I don't think I'll ever eat or close my eyes again."

Lennon: "Was there any body hurt over there.?"

Robert's: "Yes sir, one of the new men."

Lennon: "How was he injured?"

Roberts: "He fell ass over head and has a deep cut on his leg, but a few stitches and he'll be fine."

Markus: "What cut him?"

Roberts: "I think it was a piece of debris sir."

Markus: "Ok Roberts. Doc get someone to go and check them give them a full examination. I'm taking a trip to Capricorn 2 I may be able to find out what's going on."

Hughes: "I would like to request that I join the shore party."

Fox: "Where the professor goes I go."

Markus: "I can't take you with us professor, it may be too dangerous."

Fox: "we may be able to help Captain."

Markus: "I won't be able to guarantee your safety, we don't know what to expect."

Hughes: "We're willing to take that chance but we must go with you, please captain."

Markus: "Fine but if things get out of hand down there you'd better keep up. Sgt Lennon tell Roberts to report to me in the conference room then round up Ramos, Carroll, McCourt and Corporal Holland. Tell them full kit, we may be entering a hostile situation so get your men ready Sgt Gingili. Doc, I want you there with us too."

Malone: "Sir I have no combat experience I would be more of a hindrance."

Markus: "I know but we may need a Doctor. I'm not ordering you to go, I'm asking you."

Malone: "Certainly I'll go captain, my worry is I may get in the way."

Markus: "If it happens we'll deal with it. Pick up what you need and go to the shuttle bay. Tell Lennon I'll be there shortly."

As Doctor Malone left the briefing room corporal Roberts entered.

Roberts: "Sir you wanted to see me."

Markus: "While I'm on Capricorn 2 you're in charge and keep an eye on our progress. If we get in trouble get us out of there."

Roberts: "Yes captain, you can rely on me."

Markus: "Professor Hughes, Doctor Fox, after you."

A while later Captain Markus and the others were on their way to Capricorn 2. They landed the shuttle a mile outside the settlement and Captain Markus took a pair of binoculars and focused on the settlement.

Markus: "There's something strange about all this."

Hughes: "What can you see Captain?"

Markus: "Nothing, that's what troubles me, it's quiet, there's no one on the streets, there doesn't even seem to be any sort of trouble at all."

Fox: "Then it's safe to go on."

Markus: "It isn't safe, there's no people, it's a trap, we go in on the cover of night quick and quiet."

When night fell they made their way to the edge of the settlement. It seemed to be all clear. Lt Gingili looked at the map which he took from his pocket.

Gingili: "The research lab is about 100 meters that way sir."

Markus: "Ok everybody move and remember be quiet and careful."

They moved quickly towards the large steel doors but when they got there the doors were locked tight.

Lennon: "What now Captain?"

Ramos: "I could hot wire it it'll only take a few minutes."

Markus: "Get on with it."

Fox was keeping an eye out when he saw something move. He panicked and fired off three rounds into the darkness.

Holland: "What the hell are you doing?" he asked with an angry whisper.

Fox: "I'm sorry I thought I saw something."

Holland: "I swear to god if you do that again I will put you down myself."

A few seconds later they heard what sounded like a herd of cattle on a stampede coming towards them. Private Carroll spotted some sort of animal-like creatures running towards them on all fours and then a loud roar, "Kill them," it screamed. It sounded like a human voice but it was coming from one of the creatures.

Markus: "Ramos, hurry up and get those doors open."

Ramos: "I'm going as fast as I can sir."

Markus: "Well go faster then," he said with panic in his voice.

Lennon: "Sir, they're getting closer, what's your orders."

Markus: "Shoot them, shoot them all."

They opened up on the strange creatures but as quickly as they shot the creatures down they got back up. No matter how many times Captain Markus and the others shot them, the creatures got back up. All their bullets did was slow them down and piss them off.

Markus: "For Christ sake Ramos, open the freaking doors now," he shouted with a panicked tone.

Ramos: "I'm nearly there nearly there, got it," he said with excitement.

They heard the mechanism activate and the door started to open. As they backed up to the door the mechanism stopped working and the power failed. The lights went out all over the settlement and they lost sight of the creatures. All they could do was fire blindly into the night.

Ramos: "Shit it's stopped."

Lennon "It'll have to do we'll squeeze through."

Professor Hughes went first, then Doctor Fox and the others followed still shooting into the dark. When they had got through Captain Marcus looked around and saw Private McCourt firing wildly into the darkness.

Markus: McCourt, McCourt, private McCourt, calm down," he ordered with a loud authoritative tone.

Privet McCourt stood there looking out into the darkness shaking with fear then he started to laugh.

McCourt: "look Captain, we scared them off."

Markus: "Yes private, we scared them off now pull yourself together soldier and get in here."

McCourt: "Yes sir."

As private McCourt started to squeeze through the gap in the partly opened door he stopped.

McCourt: "I think my legs caught. Wait a minute. Hey. Sir help. Shit help me something's got me. It hurts."

Captain Markus immediately grabbed private McCourt by the arm and started to pull. McCourt was screaming in pain as blood started to spurt from the small opening in between the doors.

Markus: "Come on help me," he roared to the others.

Suddenly McCourt was pulled through the gap with such force that Markus was just left with a piece of material from McCourt's overalls he stepped back still gripping the blood-soaked piece of material.

Markus: "Quick Ramos, close the barrier," he ordered with a shocked look on his face.

Ramos closed the doors then sat on the ground.

Ramos: "What just happened? Oh my god sir, they killed McCourt, now we're all going to die."

Markus: "We're not going to die Ramos, we're going to find out what happened here then we're getting our asses back to the ship. Now pull yourself together we've got work to do. Let's get moving."

When they entered the facility the power switched on automatically.

Markus: "Ok people, be careful and stay together, keep your eyes open. Let's go."

As they went from room to room they wondered why there were no personnel. There wasn't even a body to be found.

Malone: "What's going on?"

Fox: "This isn't right there should be at least eighty-five personnel. Were did they all go?"

Lennon: "My guess is outside, they've become one of the mutated."

Markus: "Roberts can you read me."

Roberts: "Yes sir, loud and clear."

Markus: "The compound is teaming with the mutations but the research facility is empty. Keep this frequency open, we'll keep in contact, over and out."

Carroll: "Sir, I can't get any life signs."

Holland: "Yes we know, there's no one here," he said sarcastically.

Carroll: "No sir, you don't understand there are no life signs within the settlement at all."

Hughes: "Then that means your equipment won't give us any advanced warning of an attack."

Fox: "Or maybe they've died."

Markus: "Did you check the equipment Carroll, maybe it's malfunctioning?"

Carroll: "I've checked sir, I don't think it's the scanner but either it is the scanner or the mutations don't register on our equipment."

Markus: "We'll go to the command centre and we'll see if we can get a visual on them. Let's see what they're up to."

A few minutes later in the command centre Ramos started up the external cameras.

Ramos: "Captain, I've got a bead on a group of them."

Markus: "what are they doing? Professor Hughes, Doctor Fox take a look at this what are they doing."

Hughes: "They're watching us, they know the door we came in is the only way out. They're waiting for us to make a move."

Fox: "Wow professor, look at them they've fully mutated we never dreamed that they would be so beautiful," he said with a hint of excitement in his voice.

Markus: "What you mean, you knew about this?" he said with an angry tone.

Hughes: "No, not about this, but we knew about the infection."

Holland: "You sons of bitches, McCourt needn't have died you could've told us."

Fox: "The information was on a need to know basis and you didn't need to know."

Holland: "you piece of shit, I'm going to kill you," he roared as he grabbed Doctor Fox.

Markus: "Let him go, Holland."

Holland: "But sir, he killed McCourt."

Markus: "No he didn't, they did, now stand down."

Holland: "Yes sir." He let go of Doctor Fox begrudgingly and walked away.

Fox: "When we get back to earth Holland, I will have you up on charges, an assault on a superior is a serious offence."

Markus: "Doctor Fox, if you say another word without being asked I will order corporal Holland to shoot you in the kneecap. I'm sure he'll be more than willing to follow that order without question. Now professor, tell me everything you know now."

Hughes: "We don't know much."

Markus: "Then tell us what you do know."

Hughes: "About six months ago while the research team were examining the alien corpses one of the Doctors cut himself on a sharp sliver of bone. Over the next couple of days he started to change. He went through a horrible mutation but he still had his own intelligence so they put him in quarantine and started to study him. That's when we were called in. That's all I know, I swear Captain."

Markus: "So at that time there was only one person infected?"

Hughes: "Yes. We need to find the research notes, maybe they were close to a cure."

Malone: "Where would they have been kept?"

Hughes: "In the lower levels, that's where the labs are."

Lennon: "Then that's where the survivors may be."

Markus: "Ramos, Lt Gingili and Carroll stay here and monitor the mutants, any change in their patterns contact me straight away and keep in touch with the Orion. The rest of you follow me."

They went into the elevator and headed towards the lower levels. When the doors opened they could see a long corridor. Captain Markus exited the elevator first the others followed. They started down the corridor until they came to a security door.

Malone: "It's locked."

Fox: "This will open it," he said as he produced a key card from his pocket. Then he opened the closed doors.

Lennon: "Let's get on with it then," he said nervously.

As they reached the labs they could see through the frosted glass, bodies lying on the ground. Doctor Malone opened the lab excess door and checked some of the corpses.

Malone: "They've been dead for days."

Markus: "How did they die?"

Malone: "Oxygen deprivation, in simple terms they suffocated."

Markus: "But how did the mutants turn the air off?"

Holland: "Sir, over here, look he turned off the air to stop that." He pointed at the corner of the lab were one of the mutations was lying.

Hughes: "It must have got in as they were closing the blast doors and someone panicked then pushed the button sucking all the oxygen out of this part of the building. We must find the research."

They started to search through the computers Doctor Malone found something.

Malone: "Over here, I think this is what we're looking for."

Hughes: "Yes that's it. If you can give Doctor Fox. It looks like the file needs to be decrypted."

Markus: "Ok professor, get on with it and be quick I want off this rock as soon as possible."

Captain Marcus and the others waited when the Captains communicator activated.

Markus: "What's going on up there Gingili?"

Gingili: "There's a problem on the ship sir."

Markus: "I'll be right there. Sgt Lennon stay here with the professor and the Doctor. Corporal Holland and Malone come with me."

Markus led Holland and Malone to the elevator. A few minutes later and they were back in the control room.

Gingili: "Sir, there's something wrong on the ship, communications are garbled."

Markus: "Orion come in. Orion. Markus to Orion. come in Orion."

Roberts: "Sir, we had to barricade ourselves on the bridge. They're loose on the ship."

Markus "What's loose on the ship?"

Roberts: "The mutations sir."

Markus: "How the hell did they get aboard the Orion?"

Roberts: "It started with one of the new marines, the one that had hurt his leg on the SS Edmond, somehow he was infected. None of us saw it coming, one minute he was fine, the next he started to change, then he started to attack. We tried to kill him, but nothing we've got can even pierce his skin."

Markus: "How many are on the bridge?"

Roberts: "Sixteen of us sir."

Markus: "Has anybody been injured?"

Roberts: "No Captain, we're all in one piece."

Markus: "Bring down the blast doors and hold your ground, we'll see if we can do something from here."

Roberts: "Affirmative captain, over and out."

Ramos: Sir, Professor Hughes for you."

Hughes: "I think you better come back Captain Fox, I have unencrypted the files."

Markus: "I'll be straight there."

Malone: "He doesn't sound happy."

Markus: "Lennon, let's go. Doc you stay here and lend Gingili and the others a hand."

As captain Markus and corporal Holland returned to the labs they witnessed Professor Hughes and Doctor Fox arguing.

Markus: "What in the hell is going on here?"

Hughes: "I do apologise captain, just a little professional disagreement."

Markus: "It didn't look so little from where I was standing, now tell me what you and Fox where fighting over professor."

Hughes: "Doctor Fox refuses to give me the key code so that we can open the files."

Markus: "You said you had unencrypted the files."

Hughes: "We did, but Doctor Fox has the only operational code outside this facility to open the files."

Markus: "Fox give him what he needs now," he said with an

authoritative tone.

Fox: "No."

Captain Markus stared at Doctor Fox with one of his 'don't piss with me or I'll hurt you' kind of stare, it always worked except for this time Fox wouldn't budge.

Fox: "Don't try to frighten me captain, it won't work. The information on this computer is sensitive and top secret you do not have the clearance to see it."

Hughes: "No doctor, but I do."

Fox: "I don't think so professor, you only have authority over getting the artefacts from here back to earth. My orders are if anything goes wrong I take over, this comes straight from the top and there's nothing any of you can do about it."

Markus: "Holland, shoot Fox in the foot now."

Holland: "Yes sir, it'll be a pleaser."

Holland then looked at Doctor Fox and smiled at him.

Fox: "I told you captain, you can't intimidate me with your juvenile scare tactics."

Holland raised his gun and aimed it at Fox then he squeezed the trigger a loud bang rang out and Doctor Fox fell to the ground screaming and gripping onto his foot.

Markus: "Now give the professor the code."

Fox: "No, you crazy son of a bitch," he roared out with anger.

Markus: "Fine doc, have it your way. Holland turn him from a Mr into a Mrs."

Fox: "OK, OK here's the code," he said as he slid his data pad over to Professor Hughes.

Hughes: "Ok the files are opening, it'll take a few minutes. when it's up and ready maybe we can find out what sort of virus this is."

Markus: "You stay here, I'll go back to the control room and get doc Malone down here to take care of him, call me when you have something."

When he got back to the control room Gingili was frantically trying to get in touch with the Orion.

Markus: "What's going on Gingili? What happened?"

Gingili: "We've lost contact with the ship sir, there was some sort of interference then the signal went down. I think the ship's either gone out of range for the time being or the signal being blocked sir."

Malone: "Maybe the Orion has been lost to those things captain."

Markus: "We can't assume anything just yet. Doc, we have a wounded man in the labs go and take care of it will you."

Malone: "Yes sir."

Markus: "How are things out in the compound Private Ramos?"

Ramos: "They're doing nothing, they just seem to be waiting."

Lennon: "Sir, I think you better get down here. The professor's getting kind of agitated he keeps repeating one word, idiots."

Markus: "I'll be right there, try and keep him calm."

Captain Markus made his way back to the labs and when he got there Professor Hughes was sitting by the computer.

Markus: "Did they identify this virus professor?"

Hughes: "It's not a virus captain."

Markus: "Then what is it?"

Hughes: "It's evolution."

Markus: "Explain professor."

Hughes: "These fools knew more than they let on. They deciphered writings that they had found hidden in a number of artefacts which they understood enough to reconstruct a workable blueprint of what went on here seven thousand years ago."

Lennon: "What did they find?"

Hughes: "The structure wasn't a place of worship it was a prison and the two bodies that were found where the inmates."

Markus: "That tells us what the two corpses was doing here but not what's going on now."

Hughes: "I'm getting to that."

Malone: "I think we would all appreciate it if you would get to the point while we're all still young professor," he said sarcastically.

Hughes: "Whoever these people were, they were trying to make their species stronger by rewriting their DNA. Just think about it, no disease, the ageing process slowed to a minimum; the perfect people but something went wrong and the test subjects started to mutate it was like a forced evolution. They became violent, territorial and unpredictable and somewhere along the line they found that the test subjects were able to pass the mutation on to others like a virus."

Markus: "So the people here in the settlement, aboard the Orion and the Edmond are infected with a virus."

Hughes: "No they have gone through a forced evolution. They have gone through a million years of evolution in a matter of hours and days and the body can't handle that type of transformation. The two bodies found here were the last two survivors of the experiment. These two apparently killed the rest of the test subjects like territorial animals."

Markus: "So these people, whoever they were, built this place to hide their indiscretion, their dirty little secret."

Malone: "Or maybe to protect the universe."

Markus: "How do you come to that conclusion?"

Hughes: "The good doctor could be right if this mutation were to be let loose in a space faring civilisation it could be devastating."

Markus: "Then we destroy the site and get our skinny little butts out of here and not in that order of course."

Fox: "You can't do that, you'll destroy the discovery of a lifetime. Now that we know that there are other civilisations out there far more advanced and powerful than the human race we have a chance to be the dominant force in the universe. You're throwing away our dominance, I won't allow you to do this."

Markus: "You knew what was going on all along didn't you Fox?"

Fox: "Of course, I was ordered to bring back all relative data, the bodies and artefacts. I was to start work on my return."

Markus: "Everybody up to the control room, Fox stay where you are, I haven't decided what I'm going to do with you yet. Carroll keep an eye on him," he said angrily.

A while later captain Markus and the others entered the control room. He looked into the security monitors and he noticed that the mutants were gathering in force waiting, but waiting for what.

Markus: "How long have they been gathering like that Lt?"

Gingili: "About a half an hour sir, it looks like there waiting."

Markus: "I noticed, but I can't understand what they're waiting for. There's no way of getting in."

Lennon: "At least not that we know of sir."

Holland: "What are you thinking?"

Lennon: "Maybe the mutant in the labs wasn't one of the scientists and maybe he didn't get in when lock down proceeded. It could have got into the compound in an entrance we know nothing about."

Ramos: "There's nothing on the plans but that doesn't mean anything if there is another way in it may not be on the plans."

Malone: "An escape route?"

Ramos: "Maybe."

Markus: "Have we got back in contact with the Orion yet?"

Gingili: "No sir, not yet."

Markus: "Keep trying."

Suddenly an alarm started to sound.

Markus: "Where's that coming from?"

Ramos: "The labs sir."

Captain Markus got on to the radio and tried to contact Carroll but there was no answer.

Markus: "Ramos can you pull up surveillance on the lab?"

Ramos: "There's only two cameras working down there."

Hughes: "It's the vault captain, it's been opened, that's what set the alarm off. Private, what other camera is working?"

Ramos: "The inner vault surveillance."

Markus: "Patch us through Ramos."

They were all stunned to see Doctor Fox ingesting the dried flesh of the seven thousand year old corpses.

Lennon: "That is freaking disgusting, he gone off his rocker."

Hughes: "Can we close the vault from here?"

Ramos: "Yes, but it'll take a few minutes."

Hughes: "Then do it, do it now," he said nervously.

Ramos closed the vault door. The professor stared on with a look of horror on his face.

Markus: "What's wrong professor? He wouldn't have changed for at least a day."

Hughes: "This is different, all the others were infected through cuts with a mild infection."

Malone: "An infection is an infection, it doesn't matter how it was transmitted."

Hughes: "Wrong doctor, in this case the stronger the infection the stronger the mutation and Doctor Fox has infected himself on a massive scale so god knows what he'll turn into or how strong he will get."

Markus: "Malone, Holland and Lennon come with me we need to check on Carroll, the rest of you stay here. Lt Gingili keep trying to raise the Orion. Here Doc take this," he said as he handed Doctor Malone a pistol.

Malone: "No captain, I'm a healer not a soldier."

Markus: "Well today you're a soldier, take the gun doctor that's an order and for god sake don't point it in my direction," he said sarcastically.

When they got to the labs sergeant Lennon checked the vault it was locked up tight, Doctor Malone suddenly let out a loud roar.

Malone: "Over here, it's Carroll."

As they gathered around Malone checked Carroll's pulse. "He's dead, his neck has been broken."

Lennon: "It was Fox, that son of a bitch, open the vault I'm going to cut him a new one," he said with a loud angry tone.

Markus: "Everybody back to the control room there's nothing else we can do here."

As the captain and the others entered the control room Markus could hear a faint signal coming through from the Orion.

Ramos: "I'm trying to boost the signal sir. There we go sir, done it," he said with a hint of pride in his voice.

Markus: "Corporal Roberts, do you read me do you read me Roberts?"

Robert's: "Yes sir, were here."

Markus: "I'm glad to hear your voice now listen we're going to destroy this site, we can't risk this infection getting home how many of the crew is left up there."

Robert's: "Five of us left sir, but."

Markus: "Don't talk just listen, fire missiles five and three and destroy the S.S Edmond, then put missiles one, two, four and six on standby and program the computer to fire on these coordinates when we're free and clear."

Robert's: "Sir, I anticipated your order to take out the S.S Edmond when we lost contact and when we still had the bridge."

Markus: "You lost the bridge Roberts?"

Robert's: "Yes sir, the bridge was overrun a short while after we lost contact. When we blew the Edmond the shockwave cut our power and the blast doors opened. Then those things came ripping through the bridge crew like a shredder, the five of us barely got away."

Markus: "How did you get away Roberts?"

Robert's: "Through the air ducts sir."

Markus: "Where are you now?"

Robert's: "In the cock pit sir."

Lennon: "Well get to it, corporal," he said in an authoritative and angry tone.

Robert's: "I can't, the shockwave took out most of the instruments and we can only navigate sir. Weapons are out and so is long-range communications."

Gingili: "Restart the computers this should start all operations normally."

Robert's: "That can only be done from the bridge sir, and those mutations are everywhere we'd never get there in one piece."

Markus: "Hold on Roberts."

Markus: "Right people, what do we do now? We can't go back to the Orion, if we do we'll die for sure. We can't stay here, sooner or later they'll find their way in and we'll die."

Ramos: "Sir if we can find a way out of this compound maybe we can get to the shuttle, I know it's a short term solution captain but it may buy us some time."

Gingili: "He's right sir, it's risky but we need to get out of here and we can't fight them so we must run."

Markus: "Roberts, come in."

Robert's: "I'm here sir."

Markus: "We've got a plan. We're going to find a way out of here and get back to the shuttle it'll buy us some time. When we get near the Orion maybe we can do something from the outside to clear the ship of the mutants."

Robert's: "It won't work captain, two of us have been infected, we only have three to four hours left at the most."

Markus: "I'm sorry Roberts, there must be something we can do."

Robert's: "There is nothing you can do for us but there maybe something we can do for you. We're putting the Orion on a collision course with the settlement on the planet, we can give you three hours, no more. At that time we go into free fall whether you're off the planet or not. You're right captain, we can't risk this plague getting back to earth and captain it's been a pleasure serving with you, over and out."

Markus: "I feel the same way Roberts, good luck and god speed."

Malone: "We have to stop them captain, they're throwing their lives away, there still maybe something we can do."

Hughes: "Captain, what do we do?"

Markus: "We get the hell out of here as fast as we can."

Malone: "But what about Roberts and the others, we have to do something."

Markus: "Get a hold of yourself Doctor Malone, there is nothing we can do now start looking for medical supplies and food. Professor give him a hand."

A short while later Ramos entered the control room shouting, "I found it, I found it."

Lennon: "Well out with it, where is the hidden entrance?"

Ramos: "Below us."

Markus: "There is nothing below us but the labs."

Ramos: "There's nothing on the plans, that's true, unless you follow the elevator shaft. It goes down so far I suspect there may be a lower level and if there is, I can reprogram the elevator to take us down."

Markus: "Are you sure about this Ramos?"

Ramos: "No sir, not completely."

Gingili: "Not sure, what do you mean not sure?" he said nervously.

Markus: "It's all we've got, let's get to it."

Holland: "Sir, I think we would be wise to move sooner than later, look."

Captain Markus and the others watched in horror as they saw the severely mutated Doctor Fox ripping the vault door apart.

Malone: "Look at him, this isn't possible nothing human could do that."

Hughes: "He's no longer human."

Markus: "I think it's time we got our shit together and got out of here. Get the supplies together and head for the elevator."

They piled into the elevator as quickly as they could and when the doors closed Ramos let out a sigh.

Gingili: "What wrong with you Ramos?" he asked worriedly.

Ramos: "I forgot to mention one thing."

Malone: "And what's that?"

Ramos: "The elevator has to stop on the same floor as the lab. That's the only way I can trigger the override for us to get to the next floor."

Markus: "And you waited till now to tell us this?"

Ramos: "With all the excitement sir, I must have forgotten."

Lennon: "What do we do now?"

Markus: "Guns at the ready people."

Holland: "Our weapons can't kill it sir."

Markus: "I know, but they may slow Fox down until Ramos can get this thing moving again. Now remember be ready, but for god sake be quiet."

When the elevator doors opened they were relieved to see that the hallway was empty. Ramos got straight to work and a minute later Ramos gave the all clear. As the doors started to close a large claw-like hand reached into the elevator and grabbed Lt Gingili by the head and squeezed. Gingili's head exploded with the pressure and blood and brain matter splattered everywhere. Lennon raised his gun and started to fire at the mutant and Doctor Fox pulled his arm out of the way of the elevator doors. The elevator headed down and then suddenly stopped. The doors opened and Captain Markus and the others stepped out. In front of them they saw several drums of fuel and five high speed hover bikes."

Markus: "It's time to get out of here, get on to the bikes and let's go."

As they walked towards the hover bikes the elevator exploded into a million shards of sharp pieces of scrap metal flying through the air like high speed knives puncturing some of the fuel drums. Captain Marcus fell to the ground with the force of the blast and as he got back up he looked around he saw the mutant Doctor Fox ripping Corporal Holland limb from limb and while Holland was still screaming Fox sunk his large serrated teeth into the corporals face and started to feed of him. Markus reached for sergeant Lennon and rolled him onto his back but Lennon was dead. A large sharp piece of metal protruded from his face and Doctor Malone was missing. Suddenly he could hear someone call his name.

Ramos: "Captain, get to the hover bikes quick."

Captain Markus, Ramos and Hughes started up the bikes. Fox started to run towards Markus and the others, Ramos threw a grenade behind him as they sped down the dark tunnel.

As Fox ran after them the grenade that Ramos had thrown exploded. The explosion turned the leaking fuel into a ball of fire that went rumbling down the long dark tunnel and engulfed Fox.

A few minutes later, Markus and the others came to the end of the tunnel.

Markus: "Where's Fox?"

Ramos: "He burnt up in the tunnel."

Hughes: "Any idea where we are Ramos?"

Ramos: "The shuttles a half a mile north of here professor, we walk from here, the bikes are almost out of power."

As they started to walk they heard a noise coming from the tunnel. Markus looked behind him and as he did a scorched and burnt Fox came leaping from the darkness then fell dead at Markus's feet.

Ramos: "Sir, are you alright."

Markus: "I almost needed new shorts there but I'm ok," he said while taking a nervous gulp. "Let's go before anything else happens."

They eventually arrived at the shuttle where everything seemed quiet. Ramos opened the door.

Markus: "Let's go professor, we've only got five minutes before the Orion starts it's free fall."

Markus and Hughes entered the shuttle. They closed the door behind them and Ramos turned the shuttles floodlights on. They were shocked to see dozens of the mutants standing in front of the shuttle.

Hughes: "Why are they just standing there like that?"

Ramos: "It doesn't matter, we're leaving let them stand there."

Ramos punched in the code to start up the shuttle and nothing happened. He tried again, still nothing. Then the colour drained from his face he sat back in his chair and let out a deep sigh.

Markus: "Now what's wrong Ramos?"

Ramos: "There's no power getting to the engines."

Hughes: "Well, fix it."

Ramos: "I can't, the fuel cells have been removed."

Markus: "How do you know?"

Ramos: "Look out of the window, it's McCourt he didn't die he turned."

As they looked out they saw what was left of McCourt holding a large power cell out in front of him.

Markus: "There must be something we can do."

Ramos: "It doesn't matter now time has just run out even if we could get this crate off the ground we wouldn't escape the blast. It's been nice knowing you folks," he said with a smile.

2110: May 2. Deep space star ship Mars.
Officer in charge: Captain Paul Bell.
Classified: message to high command.
Re: investigate Capricorn 2.
Scanned area S.S Edmond lost no sign of S.S Orion.
Settlement on Capricorn 2 totally decimated.

2110 May 3 deep space star ship Mars.
Officer in charge: Captain Paul Bell.
Classified: message to high command.
Re: Further investigation of what's left of S.S Edmond.
One hour ago we found a cryogenic pod occupancies one male
horribly disfigured request further instruction.

Classified: message from high command.
2110 May 5:
Urgent lock pod down return to earth for immediate examination.

END

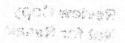